Song Of The Red Wolf

The Tala Chronicles

A Ghost Story

BOOKS BY TONI HOUSE

The Tala Chronicles

Song Of The Red Wolf

Red Mahogany
(this title may change)

Red Moon Rising

Winter Snow

The Song of The Red Wolf is full of breathless surprises that take you into chaos and mayhem, deep into Tribal Indian territory and century's old murder and vendetta's. It will keep on the edge of your seat. ~ *PW Author*

...."House does an admirable job of setting the scene in rural Alabama, and Southern colloquialisms abound, in phrases such as "hot and humid as a toad's back," an apt description for the Southern summer weather....

....The Franks are certainly likable characters, and the appearances of Chief Running Blood are scary and truly creepy." ~ *Kirkus Reviews*

"Fun-loving characters and unexpected events make this story a must-read. The sequels are bound to be as enticing." ~ Deanna Noga

"Definitely a unique and intriguing story, filled with unexpected twists and turns it will keep you turning the pages. With characters you are sure to relate to and love. The sequels are bound to be as exciting and scary as book one." ~ Columbia Review

"As Entertaining a ghost story whether it's true or not as you are likely to
read." - Decatur Review

"Characters you will fall in love with, evil ghost you are sure to hate all with true Southern Charm." - HBReviews

Song Of The Red Wolf

The Tala Chronicles

A Ghost Story

Toni House

Source Books©

A Division of SYMSYF Publishing, LLC©USA

First Published by *S Source Books© SYMSYF Publishing, LLC©*

USA, September 2015

Copyright © 2015 by The Tala Chronicles, SYMSYF and Toni House

All rights reserved. Published in the United States by *S Source Books©, a division of SYMSYF Publishing LLC©.*

The Cataloging-in-Publication Data is on file at Library of Congress.

LCCN 2015908624

ISBN: 9780996161701

Book design by Jennifer McGuire
Book Interior design by Jennifer McGuire
Book Cover design by Jennifer McGuire
Cover art by Faith Elizabeth Art

www.tonihouseauthor.com

www.housebookreviews.com

Printed in the United States of America

Distribution: Ingram

Please send your comments to MarketingSourceBooks@gmail.com

https://www.facebook.com/ToniHouseAuthor

ACKNOWLEDGEMENTS

With great thanks to the readers!
With love to my daughter Ashley, to my parents, Bill and
Eloise, and my sister and brother, Karen and Ken. And thanks to
the team that helped put this book together, to my book and
cover designer, Jennifer, Andrea McKay and to my editors.

Every seed is awakened and so is all animal life. It is through this mysterious power that we too have our being and we therefore yield to our animal neighbours the same right as ourselves, to inhabit this land.

- Sitting Bull

Song Of The Red Wolf

The Tala Chronicles

A Ghost Story

Song of the Red Wolf:

The Tala Chronicles

A Ghost Story

The First Book of a Three Book Series

Prologue

Red Wolf paused at the edge of the clearing, clad only in buckskin and a thin sheen of sweat, the full moon having guided the path of his leather moccasins. He was a young brave and full of pride as he sought to meet his chief. He was nearly six feet tall, lean and well-muscled from his active days hunting deer in the Alabama Territories with the rest of the Mecklesh clan's fierce warriors.

By his side panted Tala, his companion, watchdog, and best friend. The wolf was enormous—easily the size of two—and walked in the humid summer night, inches from her master's long, bare legs. They made quick progress from the campsite, escaping unnoticed, just as he'd been instructed.

"Tell no one," Chief Running Blood had warned him just after supper, pulling him to one side and pinning him with his cold, black eyes. "The warrior code must not be broken, and silence is to be valued above all else."

Red Wolf nodded, eager to please his chief. Now he wondered what could be so important as to warrant a private audience with his tribe's fiercest leader. Next to him Tala tensed, coat standing on edge.

Red Wolf spotted Chief Running Blood's profile in the moonlight. He paused at the edge of the forest, watching in silence as his tribal chief waited with one knee against the rock formation jutting at the edge of Dead Man's Cliff.

"Stay," Red Wolf whispered to Tala, stroking her rust-colored haunches and feeling the tension just beneath the surface. "There is nothing to fear." He chuckled. "You worry too much."

"Come," said Chief Running Blood from the shadows, his voice stern and low as his dark eyes fell upon the pair. "And leave the beast behind. I thought I told you to come alone?"

"Y-y-yes," Red Wolf stammered, bolting from the trees and glad that Tala hadn't followed him to the edge of the cliff.

Running water from a small waterfall splashed far below, turning into a fine mist as it crashed along the jagged rocks that lined the river bottom.

Chief Running Blood looked into the trees, his expression bitter with anger as he scowled at Tala. The massive beast snarled in response. When Red Wolf turned back to his chief, Chief Running Blood was smiling; a rare crack across his fearless leader's heavily lined face.

"I remember when you rescued that pup years ago," Running Blood recalled, voice thick with the memory. "We had just slaughtered her entire family."

"Everyone wanted to leave the pup behind," Red Wolf said, following his chief's eyes as they met Tala's. "But I could not bear to let it die alone in the wild."

Chief Running Blood turned back to Red Wolf, eyes cold above his fixed smile. "As I recall we called you 'Little Feet' back then."

Red Wolf blushed at the memory; many years had passed since anyone had called him that. "But once the wolf started to grow and her coat came in blood red, your name changed with her."

He nodded, pleased that his chief would remember a story about a young brave such as himself. When Red Wolf turned from Tala again, Chief Running Blood was staring at him, head cocked so that his long braid slid across his shoulder.

"You have always been rather sensitive for a brave," his chief said, the sound of scorn in his voice.

Red Wolf hung his head, no need to reply.

"I hear you do not agree with my attack on the white settlement tomorrow." His chief spat out the pine straw he was picking his teeth with.

"No, no," Red Wolf said, finding Chief Running Blood standing now, nearly a head taller and twice as wide. He was old but not ancient, and his skin seemed to be made as much of leather as of hide.

"Other braves came to me saying you did." He was circling Red Wolf now. A necklace made of the teeth of his victims danced around his neck, rattling off his rock-hard chest as the old man paced and circled. "Are you calling them liars? Or just me, Red Wolf?"

"Them! You! No, I...I am sorry, Chief Running Blood." Red Wolf bowed his head, flexing his shoulder muscles, tense from the threat of implied violence in the air. "I...I did not mean to question your leadership."

Chief Running Blood paused, and the teeth hanging around his throat clattered. "White men cannot be trusted, Red Wolf."

"Not all of them, Chief, but—"

Chief Running Blood reached out, grabbing Red Wolf's throat. His grip was tight even when Red Wolf clutched his fingers, trying to tear them off his throat. "All of them, Red Wolf. And tomorrow we will rain down vengeance on their settlement for what they have done to our people."

Red Wolf grunted, losing his grip as Chief Running Blood lifted him up and off the ground. "A pity, then, you will not be here to see your people rise up against our oppressors!"

The sound of rushing water beat in Red Wolf's ears as he felt the cool spray on his back. Chief Running Blood was dragging him to the edge of the falls. "No!" he managed to gargle, kicking out his moccasins as Chief Running Blood tightened his grip.

Tala's howl filled the night as her paws tore across the muddy earth at their feet. With a fierce growl the savage beast tore into Chief Running Blood's arm, yanking it off Red Wolf's throat as the young brave fell to the ground.

Chief Running Blood screamed as the wolf ripped at his arm, blood gushing from the wound as his chief kicked and howled into the night. As they wrestled at the edge of the cliff, Red Wolf struggled to yank Tala off his chief.

"No, Tala!" he screamed. "NO!"

But the wolf would not be denied. She dragged Chief Running Blood across the ground, her bloody snout buried in the old man's shoulder. Red Wolf grunted as his feet were yanked out from under him.

Chief Running Blood, with his free hand, grabbed the young brave's leg and would not let go. No matter how Red Wolf kicked and screamed, his chief's grip was as hard as the rocks they wrestled on.

Red Wolf looked up, feeling more mist on his face. The edge of the cliff was nigh. He reached for anything to grab on to, finding only dirt and grass beneath his trembling fingers. "Tala!" he screamed, but it was no use. The wolf would have her vengeance on the one who wronged her master.

The wolf bit down harder and harder, and Chief Running Blood screamed as he struggled to keep his balance. Then Red Wolf heard a yelp, and looked up to see Tala's hind legs scrambling to keep purchase on the wet rocks at the fall's edge.

A flicker of fear danced in Tala's eye. Her snout still clenched around Chief Running Blood's arm, and then she was gone, her rusty red coat disappearing over the edge.

"NO!" screamed Chief Running Blood as he was yanked across the wet ground, body rushing along the rocks as he and Tala fell.

Red Wolf grunted, being drawn over as well. His hands dug furiously into the ground until there was nothing to dig into and only rock beneath his wet, bloody fingernails.

"Red Wolf!" Chief Running Blood hissed from below. "Do. Not. Let. Go!"

Red Wolf risked a glance down, to see both Chief Running Blood and Tala hanging from his leg. He felt something yank free in his hip as the leg dislocated itself from the socket, and a scream gurgled in his throat as his fingers desperately grasped at the rocks.

Even as he clung, fingers slipping with each howl from Tala's snout or whimpering from Chief Running Blood, Red Wolf knew he was losing ground. The weight on him was too heavy, the rocks too slippery, and before he could prepare himself for the great journey beyond, he felt them slipping away.

Only when they were free-falling, dropping from the sky, did Chief Running Blood release his grip. Howling into the night, the old man cursed his fate and bellowed, "I will get my revenge!"

Too soon their bodies met the jagged rocks below, silenced forever beneath the flowing waters of Wolf Creek. Their shattered bones and bleeding skin became one with the great spirits, never to breathe again…

Chapter 1

The graveyard teemed with life even among the dead.

Isn't it funny—or is it sad—how, after a tragic death, life continues to move on?

Wizzie Frank knelt in the graveyard at dawn in front of her parents' tombstones. She brushed the grass clippings and dirt away with her hand and placed a small bouquet of flowers in the brass cups at the foot of each headstone for her parents and grandparents. Two generations were buried here, she thought, and both her parents and grandparents had died mysterious, untimely deaths. She looked off into the distance and a magpie caught her eye as it landed on the fountain in the center of the cemetery and flapped its wings in the cool water. She wondered where its mate could be.

The wind blew her long hair about her face. Mockingbirds sang their early morning song like everything was right in the world. She paid no attention to them or the squirrel foraging for nuts on the tree limb that hung above her head. The sound of a lawn mower ran in the distance, and she heard people laughing somewhere behind her. An unusual-looking black truck sat across the street from the cemetery as if it were waiting for something or someone.

Maybe her parents would not be too disappointed with her, she thought. Even while coping with their deaths she finished college, raised her younger sisters, Eve and Lily, and married Billy. Lily, six years younger than Wizzie, walked to the beat of her own drum and should have finished college by now. Eve, the baby of the family, would start college in the fall.

Wizzie wiped a trickle of sweat that ran down the side of her face with the napkin she took from her pocket. It was already hot and humid, she thought as she fanned herself with her hand.

She wondered what lay ahead for them all. She believed down in her bones that her family was cursed by a hidden dark secret, by something to which she had never been privy.

It had been seven years since Eve, then only twelve, found their parents dead early one morning in their bedroom. Seven years before that, almost to the day, their grandparents had died in a boating accident on the Alabama River. An unseasonable storm sank the paddle wheeler they were on, drowning all seventy-two people on board including the captain and crew. A newspaper article Wizzie found said the captain was to blame for not paying heed to the weather warnings, but there were no warnings. The storm came from nowhere, and disappeared as quickly as it had appeared.

Wizzie looked at her watch. She needed to get back to Billy who would be waiting for her, and she smiled a little at the thought of him. They were still looking to buy their first home together. *Life goes on —it doesn't seem right.* Wizzie stood and blew a kiss toward the graves, and whispered that she loved them.

"Please don't judge me too harshly," she whispered. "I'm doing my best."

She knew her parents would be happy that the three girls were living some sort of life, but they wouldn't be too happy about the fact she still had not let it go. Wizzie never believed the stories about their deaths. And no one would ever tell her any different.

Chapter 2

Billy Frank sauntered out of the apartment and locked the door tight behind him when he heard Wizzie pull up and park. It wasn't a bad neighborhood per se, but all their belongings were inside and some of them were priceless.

Well, to him and Wizzie anyway. And if truth be known, Billy had had a bad experience with his best friend while in the Army—he stole what little Billy had—so trust was something Billy didn't give lightly.

The blazing Alabama sun ricocheted off the windshield of their old Chevy truck. Billy strode across the sidewalk, pulling on the brim of his John Deere cap to shield his eyes. It was a hot and muggy day in July, but the morning held promise—and in more departments than just the weather.

Some days, all Billy wanted was to get out of this apartment and find a home he and Wizzie would share. A proper home for family with plenty of room for Wizzie's figurine collection, and a screened porch for lazy summer evenings, backyard barbecues watching the fireflies dance, and romantic rendezvous with his beautiful wife.

In their two years of marriage they'd come a long way, working hard for every dollar, hoping that a new home would soon be in their future. Their savings account was getting full enough it was time for a down payment; now all they had to do was find a house worth plunking down all that money for.

Not that Billy and Wizzie hadn't tried to find a new home but the options in Decatur, Alabama were limited, and the couple had decided it was time to venture farther south in search of their dream home.

Wizzie leaned against the rusty door of the pickup, giving him her famous smile, but today it didn't reach her eyes. Billy could see a touch of sadness behind them, and he knew to give her a little time. She was always like this after she came back from visiting her family. He paused, as always, to get a better look. Her long blond hair, slightly windblown and a little sweaty which caused curls to form around her face, whisked over one shoulder, draping down toward a blue gingham sundress that accentuated her enviably perfect figure. Billy adjusted his glasses and whistled, picking up the pace as he jogged toward her, a wide smile spreading across his face.

"Ready to go, darlin'?" he drawled, wrapping his arms around her tiny waist and scooping her up in a bear hug. She smelled like banana puddin' and sunshine.

Wizzie smiled and leaned into his embrace. She stood on tiptoe so her five-foot-three-inch frame could at least try to match Billy's nearly six-foot stature. She wrapped her arms around the back of his neck, and scrunched up her nose.

"It's such a long drive and what about my job?"

Her job was a hot topic, one he wanted to avoid at all costs today.

She whined, even though she knew he hated it when she pulled the diva card. "Are you sure you want to look all the way down in

Camden? I'm sure there are houses here in Decatur that we haven't looked at yet. And my family's here."

Another hot topic to avoid today.

"The realtor is expectin' us, Baby Dolly. And technically, the house is south of Camden in a little community called Mystery Acres," Billy said in his low, southern drawl, his voice softening. "But I promise if you don't like anything that we look at, we will keep looking closer to home."

She looked around him, and saw the truck again in the back corner of the parking lot.

"What are you looking at?" Billy asked.

"Did you see it, just over there?" She pointed. "A truck, a black truck." She looked again and it was gone.

Billy glanced over his shoulder. "There's nothing there. Now don't change the subject."

He bent his head and placed a gentle kiss on her nose, then nuzzled and breathed ever so lightly near her ear. It was a dirty trick, but it worked every time. Wizzie's lips popped out into a sensuous pout. She slowly nodded and met his eyes, her own taking on a flirtatious spark.

"I will hold you to that, Mr. Frank."

"Yes, ma'am." Billy's smile broadened again, his voice dripping with pure Alabama honey. He always knew how to make her feel better and how to get his way with her.

Without removing one arm from around her waist, he reached over and yanked open the creaky truck door. The old Chevy moaned and groaned as they piled in, crotchety as an old man being awakened from a nice, long nap. It sputtered forward out of the parking lot, filling up the silence with its constant wheezing chatter.

Billy could hardly contain his excitement as every mile brought them closer and closer to their destination. He had spoken to the realtor twelve times over the last week and had finally struck gold.

Most of the homes they'd looked at in Decatur were small and bland. Sure, they might work for now, and were a far cry better than the tiny two-bedroom apartment they'd been sharing for the last two years, but Billy knew Wizzie wanted something better.

She wanted a home, not a house. Heck, they both did. They wanted roots; a place to decorate for the holidays and invite friends and family over with pride, a place Wizzie's two younger sisters would feel comfortable calling home, too.

Now was the time to put down roots and grow their lives together and invest in their joint future.

So when Billy received a surprise email about one of the historical homes in Mystery Acres, Alabama that had come on the market, nestled right alongside the historic Alabama River, he simply could not resist and had contacted the realtor he had been working with.

If they were lucky, it would hit perfectly within their price range. *If we're lucky, that is,* Billy mused again to himself. He chanced a glance at Wizzie, and found her eyes already on him, studying his furrowed expression with concern and curiosity.

"Do you want to tell me?" she asked with a knowing kind of matrimonial authority. His pause solicited a cheeky grin. "Not having second thoughts about your promise, now are ya?"

"Now, Mrs. Frank, you know I always keep my promises. If we were not on a time schedule I would fully take advantage of that little blue sundress you are wearing."

Wizzie blushed. "In the truck?" she squeaked.

"Oh, Baby Dolly," he drawled. "That's half the fun."

He chuckled and followed the realtor's directions to the tiny town of Mystery Acres. It was a town straight out of history—*ancient* history. The streets were deserted, storefronts empty and windows boarded up.

"What happened here?" Wizzie asked as they drove down Main Street, marveling at the shuttered windows and ancient cars.

"Tornadoes." Billy sighed.

In March, 1913, one of the country's worst recorded outbreaks of tornadoes destroyed the town and left its few remaining residents reeling from the enormity of the task of rebuilding. They were passing through a desolated stretch of what was once a beautiful southern town.

"What would we do here?" Wizzie asked skeptically, watching as a stray dog limped past a series of shuttered storefronts. Billy noted she inched across the large bench seat of his pickup truck to be closer to him.

"Do what we always do," Billy said. "Make do. There's a processing plant up the road that's always hiring, or I could pick up a few night shifts as a security guard at the boat manufacturer downstream."

"Where would I work, Billy?" she whispered.

"From home, Baby Dolly." He smiled.

Wizzie inched even closer, slapping him on the arm. "What would we do for fun?"

He gave her a cockeyed, leering glance and said, "What would two randy newlyweds do in a deserted southern town for fun? You have to ask?" He winked at her.

She giggled, and the sound reassured him they could be onto something big. For so long he'd lived in cities, or at least big towns, with the same strip of gas stations and convenience stores and department stores and chain restaurants.

He wouldn't mind a place with a sense of history, with ancient buildings half torn down and all abandoned, with one post office and a couple of churches and not much else.

He felt like he got that as he drove down Highway 31 South, passing sagging houses with rusty tin roofs, spacious front yards and miles between neighbors.

A huge gust of wind came from nowhere. It shook the truck and rattled the windshield and blew the poor old truck sideways. Wizzie braced her hands on the dash, the sound of metal ripping like fingernails on a chalkboard that sent goose pimples all over her body. Heavy timbers crashed together. The ringing in her ears was deafening and her heart raced.

Billy stopped the truck short, throwing Wizzie backward into the seat. A dead tree had fallen across the road right in front of them. Then at once it was sunny and beautiful again, just like they had entered an alternate universe.

"Billy, what happened?" Wizzie whispered, almost in tears.

"It must have been one of those dirt devils you hear about."

"Right?" she snapped.

Billy pulled her close to him and kissed her pouty lips.

"Billy, turn around," she whispered. "I told you this was a bad idea."

"Wizzie, we are not too far away from where we are going. I'll just drive around the tree. You will see, everything will be fine."

Chapter 3

Billy pulled right onto Shady Acres Drive and could smell the Alabama River, rich and ancient, in the air.

"Smell that?" he asked, almost to himself.

Wizzie murmured, holding her nose, "It smells like dead fish." She turned and looked out the window and watched the landscape go by, rich and green and fresh.

"Here we be, Baby Dolly," Billy crowed, slapping his thigh as he spotted the numbers "1675" on a private lane marked Deer Run Ridge. They turned onto the gravel drive that seemed to stretch forever, bordered by miles of lush green manicured lawn like you would see leading up to a large plantation house on a TV show. Wizzie gasped as she saw the house for the first time.

"It's enormous, Billy," she said, both hands creeping toward her mouth in amazement. "How are we ever going to afford it?"

"See, I told you, Wizzie, just hang with me. I asked that fussy realtor if the numbers were right," he said, spotting her fancy Lexus parked smack-dab in front of the porch. "She said I wasn't seeing things!"

Wizzie wasn't joking; the house was huge. Large columns lined the front porch of the massive two-story home. It had a fresh coat of white paint and featured a wide widow's walk on the second floor with a matching wraparound porch on the first that looked like it circled the whole darn house.

"And right on the river?" Wizzie marveled, sliding from the passenger seat before he could race around and open the door for her.

"I believe that realtor lady said there's even a dock!"

"You made it," said a voice from the front porch. Billy turned from admiring the lush green landscape surrounding the house to find their realtor, Carol Washburn, sliding out of a front porch swing, the kind he hadn't seen in ages. "I was worried I'd given you the wrong directions."

"Are we late?" Wizzie asked with a tone that implied it wasn't a question and that, no, they most certainly were not.

"I've got 2:58 on my watch," Carol said.

"That's good; we had to dodge a dirt devil and a tree on the way here," Wizzie said. The realtor frowned at her words.

"Now, Baby Dolly," Billy cautioned her as they crept up the steps, "we're right on time. And what's wrong with a little excitement?"

Carol stood stock-still when she saw the both of them, thinking they both must have come out of a romance novel. Billy was fit and trim, with black hair, tanned skin emphasized by his white polo shirt, and snug jeans that fit his long legs and taut rear. He was attractive in a rugged sort of way, and any woman's dream and a southern gentleman to boot. His wife, Wizzie, was just as pretty as he was rugged and outdoorsy, with a tiny waist, long blond hair and big grass-green eyes.

Carol was a sturdy woman with short blond hair and big red earrings. She wore a black skirt to match the blouse beneath her forest green Washburn Realty blazer, and held a crisp leather notebook.

The realtor shook their hands. "First impressions?" she asked before opening the door.

"Marvelous!" exclaimed Wizzie, the recent events forgotten, ruining Billy's purposefully stoic face.

"I'll reserve judgment until we see inside," Billy bluffed, not missing the way Carol and Wizzie winked at each other.

He knew he wasn't fooling anyone as they stepped inside the house. It was as impressive as the outside. The hardwood floors were polished to a rich, dark shine, there was a spiral staircase leading up to a second floor that rivaled the first, and there was an impressive view of the Alabama River and various tiny estuaries from every window in the house.

What was not to love?

"Beautiful view, isn't it?" Carol asked, watching as Wizzie and Billy embraced while peering over the railing of the widow's walk outside the spacious master bedroom.

"The land looks ancient," Wizzie said, noting the thick vegetation and the many hidden fingerlings of tiny, wandering streams that branched off the riverbank.

"I hear tell it was Native American land back as far as the 1800s," Carol said with a nod, using her leather notebook to wave across the landscape. "All of this as far as the eye can see and lots of history out there and lots of...legends."

Her eyes met Billy's. When she winked, he wasn't sure if it was because she was joking or being serious. He was a mild history buff, with a box of books all about the Civil War back in their apartment, but he'd have to research her claims if they moved in.

As Carol led them back downstairs, Billy could hardly believe his good fortune.

All this…for $180,000? And ten percent down?

"What's the catch?" he asked Carol as she led them out the sliding glass doors to circle the wraparound porch on the first floor.

The river air filled Billy's nostrils as she led them to the pine railing and leaned against a solid column as she smiled her realtor smile. Rich green eyes, as shrewd as they were merry, fixed Billy above her grin.

"While the asking price may seem low to you 'city folk' from Decatur," Carol explained, "around here it's steep. You may have noticed driving through Mystery Acres the local economy is a little… depressed. So the price is right, and I hope the house is, too."

She let her words dance on the breeze, a soft, low, cool breeze Billy could picture him and Wizzie enjoying three seasons out of the year. On their own porch facing Wolf Creek, cocktails in hand, sitting on wicker furniture and Wizzie's come-hither stare dancing in flickering candlelight.

"So," Carol pressed, risking a glance at her watch, "what's the verdict? I'm not going to lie; I've got a few more showings lined up for this afternoon—"

"Might we have a moment in private?" he interrupted, steering Wizzie around the corner. But he knew by the look in her eyes there was nothing to discuss. She was gone, hook, line and sinker. As in love with the house he was.

Chapter 4

"Here, Budweiser!" called Booger Thompson, wagging a mossy branch as his chocolate lab came running, tongue wagging in anticipation of another round of fetch. They were dawdling on the banks of Wolf Creek, next to the old Tanner place, which had been deserted ever since Booger and his mom moved in a few years back.

It was midday, hot and humid as a toad's back, and Booger was killing time until his favorite show, *Haunted Happenings*, came on in a few hours. The July heat was brutal, even this close to the shore of the Alabama River, which cast a stiff breeze this late in the afternoon.

The weeds and loamy riverbed smelt like summer itself and Booger paused, sagging down on a log to rest his growing legs. He'd sprung up another two inches since Christmas, and already his favorite pair of jeans were creeping up to show his dirty tube socks.

His mom would have to go back-to-school shopping *again* in a month or two, and money was already tight. He sighed and wished he'd eaten a bigger breakfast that morning as his tummy growled. Budweiser came, clutching the stick, and dropped its slobbery goodness at his feet.

"Good boy," he said as the lab sat down, cocked his head and stared back at Booger with his big, black eyes. "Good boy." When Booger repeated the words the dog seemed to smile.

"So needy," Booger complained, smiling all the while as he rubbed the top of the dog's head between his dark chocolate ears. Budweiser had been his best friend ever since he got him as a puppy way back in elementary school. Now he was going to high school and Budweiser had grown big and strong.

"Big and strong and *needy*." Booger chuckled, rubbing Budweiser's ears. He sat back and dragged his camouflage backpack over his shoulders and onto his lap, dug in and grabbed a dog biscuit from the little plastic bag he always brought with him.

Budweiser lapped it up before curling contentedly at Booger's feet. He smiled and slid a lukewarm bottle of Mr. Misty cola out of his pack, twisted off the cap and downed most of it before offering the rest to Budweiser.

"Drink up." He laughed, watching Budweiser scoff down the rich, brown soda like a pro. The dog burped. "That good, huh? It's the last of it until we go home to watch *Haunted Happenings*." Booger could have sworn the dog's ears pricked up at the show's name.

Or maybe it was just Booger's own excitement playing games with his mind. For as long as he could remember, Booger had been a ghost-hunting nut. It started back in sixth grade when his teacher, Mrs. Rosenkrantz, informed her class that where they were sitting— yes, that very schoolroom at Milton Head Junior High—had been built on an ancient Native American burial ground.

Well, that was it for Booger Thompson. He'd never been to the school library before—at least, not voluntarily—but from that moment on he spent every spare moment camped out in the reference section, bugging the librarian for every book ever written on Native Americans in Alabama.

He learned all kinds of fascinating facts about how many tribes lived along the Alabama River, Choctaws, Muscogee Creek and Cherokee, brave warriors and fierce fighters and their families, driven off their land by everyone from the Spanish to the French to the earliest American settlers.

The fiercest of all were the Mecklesh Clan, a tribe of over a hundred mighty warriors led by the fearless Chief Running Blood. Booger was proud if a little freaked out to say that he and his mom lived on Mecklesh land, walking over the same hunting grounds that Chief Running Blood and his braves had hundreds of years ago.

Booger stood, slipping his backpack over both shoulders. "Budweiser, you're hunting where some Indian brave's dog probably hunted back in the day." He rubbed Budweiser on the head.

Budweiser shrugged, shaking his ears as he dutifully followed Booger through the underbrush. They still had another hour to kill before *Haunted Happenings* came on, and Booger figured they'd go check the crappie beds along the riverbank when he saw a car at the old Tanner place.

Two cars, in fact. He paused, considering his options. If he went right he could follow the bank of Wolf Creek until they came on the fish beds, which he'd already checked the day before.

"Probably nothing, right, Bud?" Booger asked his faithful companion as the dog stood at his side, ears pricked and eager to go and sniff out their new neighbors.

Booger crept left, hunching low in the scrub river grass that lined the riverbank and led all the way to the back side of the old Tanner place. It was a huge house and he'd never met the Tanners themselves, but he'd heard about how they snuck out of the house in the middle of the night to avoid foreclosure.

At least, that was the official story. Scuttlebutt in town was the place was haunted and that the Tanners couldn't put up with the sounds of Indian drums and ancient chanting that went on all hours of the day and night.

Booger had heard it, too, though none of his friends at school believed him. If he opened his window late at night, and the wind was right but not too stiff a breeze, he could hear the pounding of drums, the low echo of long-dead Indians chanting over and over again. Sometimes he'd wake up, the sun splashing across his face, head down on the windowsill, the drums and chanting having lulled him to sleep.

It wasn't as scary as much as it was spooky. Booger wondered if the new neighbors would hear it and run for the hills after a few months like the Tanners.

He saw the realtor right away. Booger knew her face from the billboards all over town. As he crouched in the bushes, she opened the sliding glass door and led an older couple out. Well, older to Booger —they looked to be about his mom's age: somewhere in their thirties.

The guy was big and muscly, with a smile Booger liked at once. His wife was smaller, with long blond hair and a nice smile, and he liked her, too. The realtor talked numbers, big ones, and Booger frowned, clutching Budweiser close to his side.

He hoped she wouldn't talk them out of buying.

Chapter 5

"You'll notice the interior lighting is brilliant on this side of the house in the afternoon," Carol was saying in a distracted voice. Wizzie lingered behind Billy, who was hanging off Carol's every word.

Wizzie smiled and tried to be pleasant, but secretly she just didn't like the woman. It wasn't her frosty blond hair or ugly green jacket or the way her big, clunky heels were scuffing up what might soon be their pretty new floorboards.

It wasn't even the way she clung to her notepad, which wasn't really a notepad, Wizzie discovered, but one of those newfangled "tablet" doohickeys where every five seconds she had to open it up and swipe her finger across it to show them both how "important" she was.

Still, there was something about her, something standoffish and a little superior and vaguely untrustworthy. Realtors were in a sticky spot these days, or so said Billy, who had a soft spot for working women, (Billy always said women should be treated like a queen and shouldn't work unless they wanted to) especially tall, blond working women. Not that she wasn't sympathetic to working women, after all she was one, too. She had always worked as an interior designer and decorator. But, there was something she didn't trust about her. As Billy would say, *she had that detective sense*, and it was in overdrive.

That being said, Wizzie knew the woman was desperate to unload this clunker of a house and get it off the market. There was a hurried tone to her voice, a "let's get it over with" strut to her step.

As Billy followed her around like a lapdog, peering into every corner and nodding and "oohing" and "aahing" about the four tier level crown molding and the marble countertops, Wizzie finally quit trying to keep up.

She was relieved when they turned a corner and didn't notice her as she lingered just off the main living room. She sighed, admiring the dark wood of the floors that seemed to stretch out forever, reaching all the way to the giant glass sliders, and floor-to-ceiling windows that surrounded the back side of the house. She had never seen anything like the fireplace that encompassed three-quarters of the far wall in the family room. It was built with some type of smooth bricks, smaller than normal size, with a unique insignia stamped in the middle, and had been painted a high-gloss dark mahogany red with off-white walls on either side. As soon as Wizzie walked in the room it stopped her in her tracks.

Carol was right about one thing, Wizzie thought as the light stretched out, long and low over another lazy Alabama afternoon: the giant sunroom was bathed in light, drenched in it from corner to corner. Wizzie could imagine lots of wicker furniture, soft cushions, and dozens of colorful throw pillows.

She'd go to the nearest Pier Imports for some fresh ideas, then track down a fabric store and find the closest matching patterns. Back home she'd make throw pillows and cushions for each chair, and curtains that matched in the front room so the two areas would flow seamlessly. A talented seamstress, Wizzie looked forward to those kinds of projects almost as much as buying the house itself.

Then around the corner a smaller room to the left of the kitchen and down the stairs had high ceilings like the rest of the house, and long, narrow walls. She walked in and, while the room looked spacious and empty, she knew once Billy got a hold of it with all his filing cabinets and lawyers' lamps and that big antique wooden desk of his, it would be a cramped and tight affair.

For now, she imagined her own office. A small desk in the corner, and some funky frames full of pictures from all the little day trips she and Billy had taken in their two years together. She could picture a jar candle flickering on a small table next to a cozy rocker where, on chilly winter evenings, she could sit all on her lonesome reading the thick, trashy romance novels Billy always made fun of her for.

Speaking of chilly, suddenly the temperature in the room seemed to drop by a good ten degrees. One minute the house felt downright balmy with all those sliding glass doors and the air-conditioning off, and the next it felt like a crisp fall day, the kind that found you racing back inside to grab a sweater off the hat rack in the foyer.

Wizzie stood stock-still in the middle of the small room, knowing good and well it had to be close to eighty-five degrees outside. She embraced herself, shivering as the light in the room seemed to flicker and dim. But when she looked up at the round light fixture in the middle of the ceiling, it looked just fine.

In the corner, just out of her peripheral vision, she saw the flicker of a shadow, moving fast. She turned her head, wondering if maybe a moth had followed her into the room, or even a hummingbird, but the shadow was gone, replaced by little more than dust bunnies and the chill that seemed to be getting colder.

Wizzie shook her head, berating herself for acting so childish. She wasn't cold, just stressed out. There weren't shadows flitting about the room, only an overactive imagination.

After all, two solid months of house hunting and going back to their cramped apartment every night could make anyone a little spooked by a cold and empty room. Even if it was the middle of the day.

It's a draft, she told herself, not daring to speak the words aloud lest Billy and that snippy realtor woman found her clutching herself and shivering in the middle of an Alabama summer day.

She chuckled, happy that she was just acting foolish, when a sound echoed in the room. Not a voice per se, but…several voices. She stilled her own tongue, mouth half open, listening closely as the echoes hummed above her head, swirling around the room.

Chanting, that's what it sounded like. A far distant chant, just loud enough to sound like it wasn't in her mind. She inched closer to the source, finding herself crowding the far corner of the room. She touched the wall gently, as if she might feel the vibrations of long ago drums that seemed to swirl through the air.

But all she felt was the off-white paint that covered the wall.

"Wizzie." Billy's voice came from behind and she whirled around, clutching her throat, to find him peering inside the room, a curious look on his face. "You all right?" he asked, taking one step inside the room before she flew into his arms, pulling him tight.

She'd never been so glad to see the old cuss in her life.

Chapter 6

Billy's head pounded as he crept down the stairs. It was their first night in the new house, and he thought he'd heard something in the living room.

Shuffling, perhaps?

Scraping?

No, it was more like thumping.

He left Wizzie in their new bed and slipped silently from the room, padding down the stairs in his slippers as the sound grew louder with each step. It was definitely a drum beat, steady and low, coming from beneath the stairs.

He rubbed the sleep from his eyes, glad he'd drawn the bedroom door shut so the pounding wouldn't wake Wizzie.

He crept forward, on the ground floor now, toward the sound of the drumming. It came from the little room beyond the kitchen down the stairs where Wizzie was looking forward to setting up a home office, the kind neither of them ever had before.

A soft red light glowed from beneath the closed door, beckoning to him. Each footstep he took toward the door, the drumming got louder and louder. And the floor beneath his feet grew colder and colder.

Even through his slippers, threadbare though they were, he could feel the cold tiles beneath his feet. He crept quietly, wanting only to silence the noise and go back to sleep. The door was there, at his fingertips, and he pushed it open.

The room glowed with a ghastly red light as Billy stood there in the open doorway, rubbing his eyes. And yet, when he took his hands away, letting them fall to his sides, the sight remained: blood oozing from the walls in the shape of ancient drawings, the kind you might see scrawled on cave walls or the sides of Indian tents once upon a time.

Crude animals, like big bears or simply drawn horses, were all over the walls. The blood that made them dripped slowly until it pooled on the tile floor where it formed more crude drawings of Indian warriors, spears in hand, running after bloody buffalo.

The room stank with the metallic iron scent of blood, thick and rich in Billy's nostrils as he turned, desperate to leave the room. The door slammed behind him, blood dripping down from the top in slow, maroon rivers that pooled at his feet.

The drumming sound increased, pounding in his head as the blood's stench filled his nose. He whirled to find its source, and saw an ancient drum, leather skins pulled taut over a hollowed tree trunk.

It sat in the middle of the floor, drenched in blood which splashed off it each time the drum sounded. It was like a heartbeat, thrumming, pounding, splashing blood with each beat, throwing it on the walls. The metallic iron smell made

Billy nauseous as he reached for the door, desperate to get out.

The pounding became louder, faster. Blood drenched the floor, soaking his slippers a sinister crimson as he pounded on the door, trying to escape. The blood stained his hands, and he could feel the warm liquid rising up past his ankles, and then up to his knees. The drum pounded, and his heart matched it with every beat. He banged on the door until at last it opened and...

Billy woke with a start. Wizzie was wrapped in his arms, her body warm and familiar. His heart pounded, his body covered in sweat. Panting, he untucked himself from his wife as quietly as he could, not wanting to wake her.

The digital clock on the nightstand read 3:27 a.m., and he knew, sure as there was cheap apartment carpet under his feet and sweat stinging his eyes, he wouldn't be back to sleep this night.

He padded from the room, stumbling into his slippers somewhere along the way, and quietly, so quietly, shutting the bedroom door behind him. He paused outside the closed door, letting his eyes adjust to the dim light in the living room. It was crowded with boxes, and he didn't want to sprain a toe with the big move in a couple of days.

As the streetlight from the apartment complex parking lot oozed through the half-closed living room blinds, he used the soft pools of light to dodge the boxes until he was standing safely in the kitchen.

Of course the durn coffeemaker was packed away days ago, so he spilled two heaping spoonfuls of cheap instant coffee in a cup, filled the mug with water and nuked it, standing over the sink and quivering while he waited. He pushed the "stop" button before the microwave could ding and stirred powdered creamer into the inky black mixture.

It was that vanilla stuff Wizzie liked, but it was better than drinking it straight.

He frowned, having poured too much in, but at this point he didn't really care. The little table for two in the coffee nook was still standing, although all Wizzie's cozy knickknacks—the salt and pepper shakers shaped like hard-boiled eggs and the matching rooster napkin holder—had been packed away as soon as they'd signed the contract on the new place.

He slunk into the seat, feeling every one of his thirty-three years —and twice that many—as he stared out the kitchen window into the parking lot below their second-floor unit. It was full of cars at this hour, each one bathed under the creepy orange glow of the streetlamps below.

He stared, unseeing, sipping the too-sweet coffee to steady his nerves. He didn't see the parking lot below or the rooster curtains Wizzie had sewn by hand, but the dream—the nightmare—that had roused him from his sleep, teeth sore from clamping on a scream.

His heart still pounded, and his hands shook on either side of the steaming coffee mug. He blinked, blinked, and blinked some more, but still he saw the echoes of his nightmare played out before him like a movie he couldn't stop, yank out of the DVD player or storm out of the theater.

He sank into his seat, glad Wizzie wasn't around to see him trembling like this, gray nightshirt covered in sweat, left foot tapping nervously in his threadbare slippers.

He could still smell the blood, even over the stench of the half-burnt instant coffee and frou-frou vanilla creamer. And the blood, all that blood. He couldn't get it out of his eyes—or his nose.

The drumming still echoed in his ears. He put the mug down, staring at his hands and, at last, they quit trembling. He was vaguely nauseous, and not just from the stench of blood in his nose or the too-strong coffee.

His stomach hurt because he was scared. Scared the dream was an omen, a portent of the doom to befall him or Wizzie if they bought this new house. That's where the dream took place, down the stairs from the kitchen where the small office was, that's where the blood was. And yet, it was too late. Money had already changed hands, a lot of it in the form of a down payment, plus the rental truck, the expensive boxes, and a hundred dollars' worth of duct tape.

He shook his head, wondering why he had the dream on this night, of all nights. Couldn't it have happened a week or two ago before the house was bought and (mostly) paid for?

He sat still, there in the breakfast nook. The darkness ebbed, the sun rose, his coffee cooled. With dawn came a new perspective, his eyes blinking in the morning light, his heart lifting.

It was just a dream, right? A new house was in their name, a dream house, and as Billy rose to meet the day, he was damned if he was going to let a little nightmare ruin the upcoming move.

Chapter 7

Wizzie first saw the boy as she stepped outside, steering the movers into the garage with the old bureau she wanted to refinish before moving it inside.

"In here, guys," she said, nodding at the burly young men as they sweated something fierce in the slow Alabama heat. A flash popped out from the corner of her eye and she turned.

"Hush, Budweiser, she'll see you."

Wizzie chuckled and walked over to the long row of bushes bordering their property. *Their* property! She would never get tired of saying that, ever!

There, slunk low to the ground, was a young boy and his dog, both looking up at her. "What are you doing down there?" she asked, helping the boy up. His hand was dirty and sweaty, as were her own.

The boy was in his early teens, thirteen or fourteen at most. He was summer tanned and dressed in grass-stained cargo pants and a faded maroon T-shirt that had the face of some superhero she didn't recognize on the front. His hair was short and brown with leaves in it from where he'd been hiding in the shrubs.

"Come on out now," Wizzie said, patting the dog's head. "I've got some fresh lemonade I was saving for the movers."

The young boy looked hopeful until Wizzie cautioned, "Of course, you'll have to earn it."

"Really?" he asked. They stood on the border of the property, Wolf Creek at their back, a hot, humid breeze wafting over them in the midday light. "I…I could help you move."

"You better," she said. "But first, tell me your name so I'll know who to sue if you break anything!"

He smiled, blushing a little, and stuck his hand out again, as if forgetting they'd already shaken. "Booger Thompson," he said proudly, pumping her hand energetically. "And this here's my dog, Budweiser, or Bud for short."

"Booger and Bud," she said, releasing his hand and pointing to the garage. "I do believe I've got some work for you both."

But it wasn't much. Just breaking down the big cardboard boxes she tossed into the garage as soon as she was done unpacking them inside. Billy's old boom box, left over from his college days, sat in the corner on a stack of mulch, blasting out golden oldies, but the kid didn't seem to mind.

She'd catch him snapping his fingers in between boxes, ruffling the chocolate lab's head and shaking his hips to the movement, as the dog wagged its tail with excitement.

"Where'd you two come from, anyway?" she asked, handing Booger an already sweaty glass of lemonade and putting down a plastic bowl full of water for Budweiser.

"We live next door," he said proudly, as if perhaps he'd built and painted the house himself. "I heard the moving truck this morning and thought you might need some help."

She smirked, one hand on the hip of her capri pants. "Oh, is that why I found you two hiding in the bushes before?"

He blushed, glass halfway to his mouth. "We…we were waiting for the right time to introduce ourselves, right, Budweiser?"

As if understanding him, the dog yipped and went back to drinking.

"Well, I'm Wizzie," she said, bowing since he had both hands on the side of his glass and had turned it up high to finish the very last drop. "And my husband Billy and I, we just bought this house."

"Congratulations!" he said after making that "ahhh" sound all boys did when they finished a nice, cold drink on a hot, humid day.

She paused, finger to her chin. "You know, Booger, you're the first person to tell me that. Thanks!"

He smirked, handing back the glass. "Budweiser and I are just glad to have some new neighbors. You won't be all fussy and stuffy if we, say, creep around the banks of Wolf Creek looking for old Indian bones or valuable stones or gold, would you?"

"Now, why would you do that?"

Booger's eyes got big, like maybe he'd spilled some beans better left in the can. "Oh no, I mean…just…it's summer, it's hot, what else are we gonna do?"

"Baby Dolly?" Billy called, just as she was going to interrogate Booger further. "Have you seen my—well, hello. Who are your new friends?"

Billy beamed, extending a big, brawny hand as Booger looked at Wizzie uncertainly.

"It's okay, Booger, he won't bite."

"Who says?" growled Billy, leaning in for a hug from his wife. "Now, introduce me to your friends." He stood admiring Booger and his faithful chocolate lab.

"I'm Booger Thompson, sir," said the young man with an air of politeness to his voice, as if he was addressing his junior high school principal or baseball coach. "And this here's my dog, Budweiser. We live next door."

"Ah, our first neighbors," he said, ruffling the boy's short brown hair. "Well, nice to meet you both. I see Wizzie here has already put you to work."

"Actually," Wizzie said, her curiosity piqued, "Booger here was just hoping we wouldn't get on his case about lurking around the banks of Wolf Creek, looking for gems and gold and…what was it you said? Indian bones?"

At her side, Billy tensed, as if she'd said some magic word.

Booger blushed once more and said, voice breaking as if he'd suddenly reached puberty, "Well, I mean, any kind of bones, really. Indian bones, dinosaur bones, you know…"

Billy chuckled, too loudly, as if trying to cover up a bad case of indigestion. "Find any good dinosaur bones lately, have you?"

"Oh, you know," said Booger, looking past the open garage door to the side hedges beyond which lay the curving stretch of Wolf Creek that fingered off the Alabama River to the north. "I found a brontosaurus jaw just over there last week"—he chuckled, pointing —"and a velociraptor claw the week before that."

"Is that so?" Billy said, joining in on the joke and dragging a big, burly elbow across Booger's shoulder. "Why don't you show me?"

"Now?" asked Wizzie as she stared at the boxes left to break down and the movers just emptying out the last of the truck.

Billy turned back to her and winked over his shoulder. "We're both due a break, aren't we, dear?"

She shook her head, slumping down on the footstool she'd used earlier to switch out a bulb in the kitchen. She was pooped, and it would do Billy good to have some male companionship for a minute.

She expected Budweiser to lope off after his owner, but instead the chocolate lab looked out toward the open garage door, uncertain, even a little fearful.

"You all right, boy?" she asked and, almost grateful, the dog pattered over and leaned his head on her knee.

She stroked the smooth part of his dark chocolate coat between his ears, feeling the dog's heartbeat all the way through his skin. Something had the poor dog spooked.

What could it be? she wondered as she watched Billy and Booger standing on the other side of the shrubs, deep in conversation. *And why was Billy taking such an interest in bones all of a sudden?* Now, if it was treasure hunting, she understood that. Billy loved to go out into the middle of nowhere with his metal detector and look for gold, because he knew one day it would find some.

Chapter 8

"Waddya do for fun around these parts?" Billy asked in his trademark southern drawl. He took a pack of gum from his worn-out jeans pocket and offered a piece to Booger, then unwrapped a piece for himself and stuck it in his mouth.

Covering Billy's thick black hair was a blue ball cap for a race car driver Booger didn't recognize because the only TV he ever cared to watch was the Scream Channel and, of course, his favorite *Haunted Happenings* program.

Booger watched his bobber float in the warm, brackish water of Wolf Creek and shrugged. "You're looking at it," he said, popping his gum. He reached and pulled a long strand of grass from the riverbank.

Budweiser lay stretched out flat in the sun with his paws over the edge of the dock, head hanging down, waiting for either of them to catch something.

"Good luck," Booger wanted to say, but he knew Budweiser, smart as he was, wouldn't understand him.

An hour earlier Booger had been standing there, minding his own business, enjoying the last few days of summer when Billy came by with a fishing pole in each hand.

"Make yourself useful," Booger's new neighbor had drawled in his Alabama twang, winking down at him and handing him the extra pole. "Maybe we can have fresh trout for dinner."

Booger shrugged. *What the heck?* he thought. It sure beat watching Budweiser fart, burp and scratch his hindquarters all morning long.

"Don't you have any friends?" Billy asked in a neutral tone. It wasn't an accusation or an insult, just a question. Or maybe, Booger guessed, more like an observation.

"Not this far out in the boonies," he said with a shrug. "Got a few pals at school, but none want to ride their bikes all this way in the heat."

Billy nodded and wiped his brow with his forearm. "Dogs are better company, anyway," he said, regarding the drowsy chocolate lab with a smile.

Booger agreed.

"Any girlfriends?" Billy asked, adjusting the brim of his NASCAR cap and grinning.

Booger blushed, thinking of Mary Sue Meyers and her long, black hair and slinky white knee socks. "No sir," he answered too quickly.

Billy arched one eyebrow and nodded. "You'll confess when the time is right." He chuckled dryly and put back on a serious face.

Booger smiled. It felt funny fishing with a man, doing anything with a man, for that matter. It had been so long since his father left them high and dry in the old river cabin that Booger hadn't had much to do with grown men after that.

That is, other than his PE coach, Mr. Marble, and Principal Dander at his school. And they weren't the kind to go fishing with him or ask about friends and certainly not about girlfriends, that much Booger knew.

Still, he thought as the bobber floated there, it wasn't half bad.

They could stand there, fishing, leaning against the dock railing, saying nothing for five, ten minutes at a time. Burp, even, if they wanted. Or fart or scratch their armpits or pick their noses and nobody could tell them otherwise.

"Think it's the right time for a beer break?" Billy drawled, scratching his butt as if he could read Booger's mind.

"Is there a wrong one?" Booger joked, parroting something he must have heard in a beer commercial once.

Billy snorted and reached into the battered red cooler at his feet, popping the tops of two cans. Booger's heart fluttered, thinking he might get his first taste of beer, right here on this very dock, in the last days of summer before ninth grade! Then Billy handed him a can of Old Farmer's Root Beer, cold and fresh, and tossed that dream right to the ground.

"Nice try." Billy smirked, letting out a chuckle as he sipped his own root beer. "Maybe next time, Booger."

Booger snorted and drank half his beer—his root beer, that is—at a pull. It was early August and he started school next Monday. You'd think it'd get a little cooler with summer almost over but, jeez, it felt hotter than mid-July, and the only things enjoying this time of year were the mosquitos.

He pulled down the brim of his faded *Haunted Happenings* cap and finished off his root beer, the sugar and the cold giving him a little lift.

"Got something," said Billy, yanking on his pole as the water thrashed with his big catch.

Booger's eyes almost popped out to see Billy's pole half bent and the fishing line taut deep in Wolf Creek. "Something big!" shouted Booger, rushing over with Budweiser close by his side, yapping away, just as Billy yanked and the line snapped free.

"Dang," they both said at almost the same time. Budweiser stared down at the water, whimpering with disappointment.

"Did you see it?" Booger asked, inching closer as Billy knelt on the dock to lean his face to the water.

"Naw," Billy said absently, face an inch from the surface of the creek. "But, durn, I lost my favorite lure." He looked up at Booger, red-faced. "Sorry, didn't mean to curse like that but…dang if that thing didn't cost me close to twenty bucks."

"Jeez," Booger said, shaking his head. "I've got a pair of wading boots if you want me to fish it out for you."

Billy stood, sweat dripping from his forehead. "Naw, it ain't your problem, son. It's mine, for using a good lure in a crap pond. I should have used catawba worms for bait, but no one sells them here. The next time I'll drive to Camden to buy them." He looked down at Booger, frowning again. "Sorry," he said with a smile, tousling Booger's hair. "Guess I ain't used to being around young people so much. I'm gonna have to start watching my mouth around you."

Booger slumped down onto the dock, hiding beneath the shadow of his baseball cap. Budweiser stood sentinel, halfway between Billy and Booger, as if the fish might poke its head up and squirt water at him, just for fun.

"Naw, Billy. What's a little fishing if it doesn't come with cursing?"

Billy chuckled, tying another lure to his line—a much cheaper one this time—and plopping it back into the creek. "I like your style, kid. I think you and me are going to get along fine. Just fine."

Chapter 9

Billy watched as Booger and Budweiser loped off for home. He stood at the foot of the dock, cooler in one hand, fishing pole in the other. When at last the two friends disappeared around the corner, the high brush of reeds that bordered the riverbank obliterating his view, Billy sighed and put his gear on the ground.

He kicked off his shoes and rolled up his jeans, though he knew it wouldn't do any good. Then he waded out into the creek, the muddy water cool as his feet sank into the riverbed.

He shook his head at his own durn foolishness, but truth be told that lure was worth a lot more than twenty bucks, and danged if he was going to lose it on his first day of fishing!

He treaded carefully, not wanting to step on an old tin can or rusty bottle cap or, heaven forbid, one of the six hooks of his beloved lure. He guided himself by the dock, knowing he'd been leaning against the fourth rail when he'd first cast his line—there, right there, something sharp and stiff beneath his feet.

He peered into the muddy water, which was made muddier by his progress. With a satisfied smile he reached down, expecting to feel the familiar shape of his trout-shaped lure.

Instead he found something sharper and longer nestled in the weeds layering the bottom of the river. He knelt, water up to his thighs now, both hands digging around carefully as he inspected the find at his feet.

It was too large to be a lure, so what was it? He wound his fingers around the slimy sides of the shape and tugged. It gave, a cloud of bubbles bursting to the surface and with it a roiling wave of river grass and mud.

When at last the shape burst free, Billy gasped. It wasn't a lure, or river grass or debris or anything he'd been imagining. It was a bone, bleached from the sun and free of all flesh. It looked like it had been there for years, decades even.

It was a thigh bone, or femur, or whatever you called the long leg bone above the knee. The hook had sunk into the length of it and, as Billy held it, he carefully slid the hook from the bone and leaned back against the dock, studying it.

As it dried it began to look more and more like something out of a horror movie, a human bone, in his hand. Found just off the dock, behind his new house.

"Man," he muttered in disbelief. "What in the world am I holding?"

He found himself, quite unconsciously, wading back to shore. He hadn't meant to, and couldn't remember deciding to, yet there he was just the same, trudging up on dry land and carefully laying the bone down at his feet. He wasn't often scared, and he wasn't now. Not exactly, but he was spooked out and for some reason, putting the bone down on the soft, loamy soil at the water's edge made him feel instantly better.

He looked around, to his left, to his right, wondering if anyone saw him and then wondering why he cared. But there was something cruel and unusual and weird and a little bit scary about finding an old leg bone buried in the creek. His mind reeled with questions:

Whose leg was it?

Why was it in the creek?

And how did it get there?

It looked old, bleached and brittle and from another era, it seemed. He wanted time with it, time to study it, to dry it out and inspect it, before he told somebody, if he told anybody.

Why should he?

Why would he?

It could be a dog bone, for all he knew. But it looked too big to be a dog bone. Maybe a bear bone? But inside he knew it was human. It had to be. It was old, older than he was, that's for sure. It could be fifty, sixty years old. No reason to stir up trouble until he knew a little bit more, right?

He felt anxious now, feverish not to be seen. He looked around, wondering how to get the thing inside without snoopy Wizzie noticing. That gal noticed everything. He always said she should have been a detective, and now she would be detecting him!

He spied the cooler; it was just about the right size, though Billy wasn't sure he'd ever want to use it again after shoving a human leg bone inside it. He gently tucked the bone inside until, like a human jigsaw puzzle, it fit well enough so that he could close the top.

Well, mostly.

Then he slipped back into his socks and shoes, and squeaked and dripped and sopped all the way back to the garage. Of course Wizzie was there, changing out the wash, when he squeaked up, and her eyes grew big as she marveled at him standing there, dripping in the driveway.

"What in tarnation?" she exclaimed, slapping one thigh.

He made a face and gestured with his pole. "I went along and fell right off the dock," he lied, a little old white lie, figuring she'd rather hear that than the truth.

"Goodness, well, get out of those wet clothes or you'll catch your death. And here I thought I was done with the laundry for today."

He chuckled as he set the cooler down, using the dropping of his shoes to cover the sound as he slid it behind the row of metal trash cans in the corner of the garage.

"Won't be a bit of trouble," he said, padding deeper into the garage on bare feet. "You run along now, whip us up some lunch and I'll toss this load in."

She stopped, wide-eyed, by the drying rack. "Did you go and bump your head in that old crick?" She chuckled. "Never in two years of marriage have you done a lick of laundry!"

"Well, now," he said, turning her around and patting her taut little fanny as she bolted for the garage door, "then it's about time I learned, right? Plus, with these newfangled washing machines, how hard can it be?"

She chuckled, wagging a finger. "Don't get cocky, Billy Boy," she warned, and disappeared into the house.

He sighed, stripping off his clothes, and dumped them in the washer before tossing in some detergent and pushing a few buttons. When it finally started, he snagged some boxer shorts and a crisp white V-neck T-shirt from the drying rack.

Then he crept back for the cooler, carrying it to the door but peeking in to make sure Wizzie's back was turned before sliding inside. She was at the sink with her back to him, washing and cutting up tomatoes for her famous roast beef and Muenster sandwiches.

He hustled down the hall, careful to avoid the squeaky spots he'd already identified in the rich hardwood floor on the way down the hall. He was going to take the bone up to the attic, but he knew the squeaking steps and his pounding footsteps upstairs would alert Detective Wizzie.

Instead he thought of the home office just down the stairs next to the kitchen, so he slunk down the narrow hallway and slipped inside. He switched on the lights, staring at his antique desk in one corner and Wizzie's craft table in the other. Every available space was littered with her fabrics and various sewing kits as she set about matching the drapes to the throw pillows to the cushions to the upholstery.

He whirled around, trying in vain to fit the cooler behind his desk. It stuck out from the desk's ornate carvings like a sore thumb. Just then the air rattled on and Billy turned, hearing the rumbling from behind the crawlspace in the corner.

He knelt, using the penknife from his desk drawer to loosen the twin screws on either side of the vent. When it was open he looked inside, finding it dark and deep and just wide enough for the human leg bone.

He opened the cooler, finding the bottom filled with silt and the unwelcome smell of hot river water wafting up. It must have dripped off the bone during his journey. He winced and slid the bone, still dripping and damp from Wolf Creek, inside the dark, dry duct, and quickly closed the vent.

Later, when Wizzie was fast asleep and he had a little privacy for a change, he would creep down here to dry the bone out and study it closer. For now, he could hear her calling for him in the garage. Suddenly famished, he stood and straightened, leaving the cooler behind for now.

Chapter 10

Billy sat down in the creaky chair and was glad for the big desk between him and the shift supervisor, Matt McLellan. That way he could wipe his sweaty palms on his finest khakis without the man noticing.

He'd never been good at interviews, or tests, or oral reports. High school had been a nightmare, and college was worse, and he'd been fortunate back home in Decatur to always get a job through a friend of a friend or, more often than not, a family member.

But here in Camden, he didn't know a soul other than Wizzie and that realtor lady, Carol, and good luck getting a call in to her once the sale was done. So he'd taken the leap and hit the want ads and there it was, one of the very first squares he circled: "Night Watchman, Plastics Factory." He could forget having a mechanics or engineering job, living here.

Now here he sat, in his crisp new khakis and the squeaky brown shoes he only wore to church and weddings (rarely) and funerals (hardly ever), trying not to wriggle the tie wrapped like a noose around his neck.

Matt McLellan was a big guy, beefy but young. He looked like he played ball in school a few years back and was fit at some point, but after a few years off the field he kept eating like he was still a teenage boy and now he was fleshy and thick.

"Know much about plastics?" he asked dubiously, staring at the application Billy had filled out.

Billy shrugged. "Do I need to?" he asked in his syrupy southern drawl. He held his breath, waiting on Matt's reaction.

Finally, Matt chuckled and slid the clipboard containing Billy's résumé onto his cluttered metal desk.

"Not at all." He sighed, leaning back in his chair and putting his hands behind his head. Billy noticed sweat stains around both armpits of his faded yellow short-sleeve shirt. "Basically you're just babysitting a bunch of big, heavy, expensive equipment all night."

Billy nodded. "I done security in a John Deere plant back in Decatur and night watchman at the feed plant before that, maintenance on large paper machines so I know my way around a flashlight or two."

Matt nodded, sucking on something between his teeth. Something from breakfast, Billy thought. Or maybe even second breakfast. Then his faint smile shifted and he inched back to an upright sitting position, beefy arms resting on his cluttered desk. "I'll be honest with you, Billy, right now the job's between you and the boss's cousin."

Billy's smile remained fixed, but he worked to hide a frown. So far, things had been going so well. "Problem is, the kid's way too young, too irresponsible, I don't trust him not to swing the doors wide open and invite his whole gang in here to party every night."

"Won't be no partying if you hire me," Billy interjected, hating the desperate sound in his tone. Matt began to speak, to make an excuse, to explain why Billy wouldn't be getting the job, but Billy wouldn't give him the chance. "Look, sir, I know you're in a tough spot. I've been there, having to choose between the right guy and the easy guy. But I tell you, I'm two years married, just bought a big old house on Wolf Creek, mortgaged up to my eyeballs, the wife down at the fabric store twice a day buying material for throw pillows to match the curtains to match the drapes. I'm new in town, got no friends, got no life besides the wife. You're not going to find a more motivated employee than the one sitting right in front of you."

Matt held up a hand, face bland, cheeks flushed. "I hear you, Billy, and I know you're right, but..." He stood, big belly fluttering the papers on his desk, beefy hand extended. "Let me sit on it awhile and give you a call back."

Billy stood and shook the bigger man's hand. "I thank you," he said, trying to keep it positive, though he knew from the man's voice he'd already made his decision. *The right one.* The right one for his career, that is.

"I'll be in touch," Matt said, showing Billy to the door.

He nodded and muttered, "Sure." As soon as he was around the corner from the office side of the building, he slid his ball cap from his back pocket and plopped it on his head, loosening his tie on the way past the receptionist.

Billy was in the grocery store picking up a few supplies for dinner, looking at Wizzie's sweet handwriting on a sticky note, when his cell phone chirped. He dropped the note in his basket while fumbling for the phone and his heart fell when he saw the words "Peterson's Plastics" in the little cellular window. He shook his head, sliding it in his back pocket. "Bad news can leave a message," he muttered to himself, sliding a can of corn niblets into his basket.

He figured Matt had waited just long enough to seem like he'd been mulling the decision, then quick dialed him just to get the weight of delivering the bad news off his chest.

The phone chirped again as Billy slid into his truck, two paper bags of groceries riding shotgun in the passenger seat. When he saw "Peterson's Plastics" again, he sighed and hit "answer."

Better to face the music, he thought, *than keep dodging calls all weekend.*

"Billy," Matt called out, voice booming through Billy's cheap two-year-old cell phone. "You're a hard man to track down."

"Sorry," he said, nervous fingers tapping the steering wheel as he sat in the parking lot. "Picking up some sundries from the market."

"Well, listen, I'm glad I caught you while you were still in town…you mind swinging back by and filling out some paperwork?"

Billy sat, stunned, blinking as a woman in rollers got out of her brand new Cadillac across from him. "You mean I got it?"

"Sure thing, bud," Matt said. "I guess your speech won me over. My boss, too. So we'll want you to start tomorrow night. Got any problems with that?"

"Heck no," Billy said, firing up the engine with his free hand. "I'll be right over."

On the way back to the factory on the other side of town, he saw a wine bar and smiled, thinking how nice it would be to drop in on his way back and pick up a bottle of wine to go with dinner to celebrate.

Chapter 11

Wizzie looked up from her sewing machine and took her foot off the pedal at the same time, stopping the machine cold. A little radio was on next to her sewing table, playing old-time country music, and she snapped off the radio harder than she'd intended.

It was near midnight and she was wired, wired from fear. It was Billy's third night working the graveyard shift at Peterson's Plastics, and even though she sent him off each evening with a bagged lunch, a sweet sticky note stuck to his Little Debbie snack cake, and a plastered-on smile, the minute Wizzie saw his red taillights pulling out of the driveway her heart sank and she shut the door, locking and checking it again just to make sure.

Then she turned on every downstairs light and retreated to her sewing room, switching on the country music to keep her company and trying to finish one project each night.

She'd never been a flighty woman, nervous or dizzy. She always considered herself quite strong. She'd raised her two younger sisters, after all—well, she raised Eve and survived Lily's rebellious and defiant personality—but she'd never lived in a house this big before, on a lot so far away from town.

She thought she'd love it, and she did. During daylight hours, that is. The house was big and bold and beautiful, a steal at the price and beyond anything she'd ever imagined owning, particularly at such a young age.

The widow's walk that encircled the second floor alone was worth the price of admission, and there was nothing Wizzie liked more than greeting the day by opening wide the French doors from their master bedroom and slipping onto the porch, leaning over the railing to watch the rippling waters of Wolf Creek. The fireplace was also well worth the cost of the house.

But at night it was a different story. The house seemed old and creaky then, the large trees that lined their property sinister and shadowed in the mist that frequently swam in from the creek, oozing past the sliding glass doors like cloudy fingers looking for an open door or unlatched window.

But the sounds, the sounds were the worst—creaking branches, croaking frogs and clicking grasshoppers and more, so much more. She found it hard to sleep, especially with Billy gone these last three nights.

So she didn't. She brewed two hot pots of coffee just before he left for his shift, one to fill his calico thermos and the other to fuel her nightly sewing activities.

She looked to the large wicker basket where she'd stacked her throw pillows all week. Five were done, with three more to go before she could start on the set for the downstairs porch.

Still, it kept her hands—and ears—busy while the night wore on. And yet tonight there was a new sound, one she couldn't ignore, though she'd been trying to since Billy left.

Howling.

Yes, she was sure of it now…howling.

It started out low and soft. The kind of sound you could easily dismiss once you reached over and turned up Reba McEntire on the radio. But even over good old Reba, the howling persisted. Soft at first, then a little louder, it was the unmistakable sound of an animal howling, like something out of a monster movie on some Halloween Fright Fest.

Now she stood, the sewing machine and radio turned off, standing stock-still in the wood-framed doorway of her little sewing nook. It was just off the den, past the stairs and between the guest bathroom and the laundry room.

All the lights were on in the living room, but all they did was cast back her own frightened reflection in the floor-to-ceiling windows. She glanced at herself, a trembling young woman in pink yoga pants and a gray hoodie to fight back the autumn chill, one nervous hand still clutching the sewing room doorway.

With the other hand she reached out and turned down the dimmers until the room grew dark, and gradually she began to see details outside the living room windows. The patio furniture was arranged just so, most bearing the new maroon cushions she'd been busy sewing all weekend.

Beyond, she could see the big mossy trees that dotted the playground-sized yard, clear down to Wolf Creek where the moon danced on the water and the tiny waves lapped against the wooden dock.

Then…the howl. Again it was almost like a scary, sad song. Not in front of her, where she was looking, but behind her, in the front yard. She shook her head, gritting her teeth, knowing she had to see what was making all that racket if she ever hoped to sleep at some point.

She cursed under her breath, creeping across the varnished floorboards as she inched toward the front of the house. She passed the fireplace, silent and dark this time of year. Billy said they couldn't light a fire until at least Halloween or it would be "rushing the season," whatever that meant, but he didn't say anything about using the fireplace tools.

She grabbed a poker, heavy and solid in her hand, not feeling the slightest bit ridiculous as she approached the front door. The howl continued, long and low. She clenched her eyes shut, shook her head, reached for the door and, before she could chicken out, flung it open.

The howling stopped immediately. It was as if the sound was on a timer set to the door. She opened her eyes, and saw the sky outside was dark but faintly lit by the half moon. Standing in the doorway, clutching the poker with one hand, she squinted and peered into the darkness.

The lots were thick and wooded back here, and not a neighbor in sight. Booger's house was far to the right, little more than a glowing window in the second floor past nearly an acre of dense forest.

She heard the howl again, closer, louder this time and longer, too. She followed it to its source and gasped. There, across the street, was a pair of fiery red eyes poking out between two trees.

"Jesus," she exclaimed, clutching her poker even as she inched closer to make sure her eyes weren't playing tricks on her. The creature stepped from the bushes and into the clearing. It was a wolf, and huge, too! Fully grown, its mane was rusty red in the dark. Maybe it was a reflection from the moon, the light playing tricks on her eyes. She'd never seen a huge red wolf before.

Their eyes locked. The wolf froze, as did the howl on her lips. Then came a slight squelch, like a squeal of surprise, and the wolf retreated, leaping away, or more like she just vanished into the dark.

Wizzie sagged as if the life had just gone out of her. Leaning against her doorway, she waited until she caught her breath and then slipped back inside, slamming the door against the dark and what lurked within it.

She was still there, panting, when the phone rang, jarring her so badly the fire poker clattered to the floor, rattling just out of reach. "Jesus!" She reached for the receiver in its cradle on the kitchen counter. "Yes?" she barked.

"Wizzie?" came Billy's voice, soft and gentle, making her want to cry with its sweetness. "Honey…are you okay?"

"Yes, yes," she lied, brightening if only for him. "I…you just startled me, that's all. I must have…must have fallen asleep while sewing."

"Oh gosh," he said, sounding upset. "I didn't want to wake you, I just…I'm on my break and wanted to hear your voice."

"How sweet," she cooed, sagging against the kitchen wall and sighing like a schoolgirl with her first crush. "I'm happy to hear your voice, too."

"Really?" he asked, sounding surprised.

She snorted, the tension of the past few moments suddenly flooding away. "More than you'll ever know, honey. More than you'll ever know…"

Chapter 12

Billy finally felt rested as he hauled his toolbox out to the back porch later that week. It was midevening and a light drizzle all day had turned the yard into a mudslide waiting to happen.

And yet the big wraparound porch was warm and cozy. Wizzie was there, dragging wicker furniture to and fro and fluffing up her homemade throw pillows just right. She had a few candles going, flickering as the daylight waned beneath the steely gray clouds. Somewhere inside, a country music station played golden oldies through the large open windows.

He smiled to see her so excited and told her so.

"I'm just glad to have you home to myself for one night this week," she said, wrapping him in a hug before he bent to his chore. "Seems like I barely see you anymore."

"Now, Wizzie," he said, chiding her. "This isn't my first night shift since we've been married."

"I know," she frowned, pausing in her pillow fluffing duties. "But it's the first one in this big house all alone."

Billy knew she hadn't been sleeping well. Partly it was to stay on the same schedule with him, so she'd be there with breakfast waiting when he got home at six and then they could still sleep together before rising later that afternoon.

But it was more than that. Her usually lively eyes were puffier than usual and circled underneath in gray. She was jumpy, too, nearly bursting out of her skin when Billy slammed the toolbox into the dining room table by accident a few minutes earlier.

"Once I get a little more seniority," he promised, kneeling to his work, "I'll get a better schedule and we can both quit living like night owls."

She nodded, brightening, and turned back to her pillows. "I won't mind being alone in this big old house as much during the day," she said absently, as if she'd forgotten he was there.

He fiddled with his hammer and found the right nails, preparing to tighten some of the loose floorboards Wizzie had been complaining about tripping over all week. "Now, what's got you so spooked while I'm gone at night?"

She turned, throw pillow clutched to her chest like a talisman, looking somewhere right above his head. "Oh, nothing," she said, with what he thought was false brightness. "Just the sounds of an old house settling, you know how it is. I'm not used to it after that tiny apartment of ours."

Billy shook his head. She was holding something back, but he knew her well enough to realize that when she was ready to talk about it, she would. For now, they were together on a Saturday night, in their new home, settled in, and all was right with the world.

That is until the barking started.

"Oh Lord," Billy muttered as he heard Booger trying in vain to hush up Budweiser.

"You hush," Wizzie warned, inching toward the edge of the porch as Budweiser splashed through the muddy yard. "They're the only neighbors we've got and Mama taught me to be kind to neighbors cuz you never know when they might come in handy."

"A thirteen-year-old kid and his mutt?" Billy chuckled, finally hammering down the first of seven loose floorboards. "How are they going to save us?"

Wizzie shushed him and tossed her pillow aside to pat Budweiser on the head. She made doggy talk with the lab while Booger crept onto the porch shyly.

"How's it going, Mr. Frank?" he asked, ball cap soaked from the drizzle.

"Good, Booger," Billy answered, starting in on the second board. He looked up. "What, no creature features on tonight?"

Booger smiled. "Not 'til later, Mr. Frank." He waited a bit before adding, "Don't worry, we won't bother you. I was just gonna go check on the crappie beds when Budweiser saw your lights on and decided to come for a visit."

Billy chuckled and smiled. "Stay as long as you like, kid. You're not interrupting anything…yet." Billy winked at his wife.

Booger blushed and slid down to one knee to watch Billy work. Meanwhile, his trusty dog dropped a muddy tennis ball onto the porch steps.

"Oh, look," Wizzie hollered, "he wants to play fetch."

Booger and Billy both turned to her at the same time. "Don't get him started, Mrs. Frank," Booger warned. "He'll play fetch until his paws are bloody."

"And muddy!" Billy said, pointing with his hammer to the mud the dog had already tracked up the porch steps.

"Nonsense," Wizzie scoffed. "That's what hoses are for, boys." With that, she tossed the ball as far as it would go. Unfortunately, it was only as far as the pond just to the left of the porch.

As if the muddy yard wasn't wet and ugly enough, sure enough Budweiser went bounding straight into the pond, barking merrily and making sure every muddy paw got twice as wet as he splashed around until he retrieved the floating ball with his teeth.

Wizzie squealed with delight until the dog came back, dumping the muddy tennis ball at her feet. "What now, Booger?" she asked as she stared at it, alarmed.

Billy and Booger both laughed. "We warned you," they said. Billy turned back to his work but watched out of his peripheral vision as she picked the ball up gingerly, fingers mired in mud and dog slobber, before tossing it right back into the pond.

"Oh no," she groaned as Booger sat back on his haunches with laughter and Billy stood to put an end to the hilarity.

"I told you not to encourage that dog," Billy said, intercepting the ball when Budweiser brought it back. The dog waited patiently for him to throw it back in the muddy pond, but Billy had a better idea.

Instead he whipped his arm back as far as he could and launched the ball over the pond, past the dock and right into Wolf Creek. Budweiser turned, tensed, muscles flexing as if to chase it, then saw it floating in the creek and whined. He inched past Billy onto the porch and shook the remaining water from his coat, soaking Billy's shirt.

Wizzie squealed with laughter. "Serves you right for throwing his ball into the crick." She shook her head and petted the dog's head as Booger grabbed his collar. "Don't mind him, Budweiser," she cooed as Booger doffed his hat with his free hand and led the dog away. "Billy's just a big old grump. You come back anytime, you hear?"

Wizzie looked over at Billy as he watched Booger lead his dog back home.

"Don't scowl at me so, woman." He chuckled, returning to his work. "I'd never get this porch done if you kept playing fetch with that mutt."

She shook her head and wiped her hands on her denim skirt. "I don't know why you're so obsessed with that porch anyway, Billy," she said, huffing inside to check her pot roast. "You're never home to use it no how!"

She closed the slider behind her and Billy could feel her stomping all the way into her new kitchen. He sighed and hammered away his frustration.

He liked Booger; he even liked Budweiser. He wasn't sure what had gotten into him either. *Maybe Wizzie wasn't the only one not getting enough sleep these days,* he thought, hammering the night away.

Toni House

Chapter 13

Booger heard the howling and, at first, he thought it was his TV. After all, his favorite B-movie of all time, *Werewolf Bikers from Mars*, was on the Scream Channel so he figured it was just part of the soundtrack.

But during a potato chip commercial? He hit the mute button, stood up and crept toward his bedroom window. It faced the side yard, and on clear nights he could see a sliver of Wolf Creek out in the backyard.

He peered out the window but, with the TV set on, all he could see were flickering reflected images. He used the remote still clutched in his hand to turn it off.

Once his eyes adjusted to the dark, the full moon illuminated the backyard, cluttered with a half-built tree fort, a skateboard he'd been trying to fix, and other various fads and hobbies he'd pick up and put back down every week or so.

He was staring at an old desk chair he was going to make into a haunted house ride last Halloween when he heard the howl again. This time, in his silent room with the TV off and his mother having long since passed out in her bed, the sound was quite clear and distinct: a wolf howl.

But not out back, like he'd thought, but on the other side of the house toward the front. He slid on his jacket that he always slung on one of his bedposts and slipped into his flip-flops by the door.

He poked his head out into the hall, the nightlight in the hallway bathroom the only illumination in the darkened house. He crept down the hall, past his mother's room where, through a half-open door, she snored fitfully, twisted in her sheets from another bad dream.

He worried about her, all alone after Booger's dad left them, but what could he do? His best, he figured, as he shut the door behind him and inched closer to the front of the house.

Another howl, louder this time; he was moving in the right direction! He wasn't sure why that made him happy, but for some reason it did. He unlocked the door and slipped onto the front porch, peering into the night.

It was cool, but not chilly, making Booger wonder why he'd grabbed his jacket. He stood stock-still as the full moon illuminated his mom's five-year-old sedan in the driveway and the empty street just beyond.

He heard the crackle of leaves to his left, and turned just in time to see a shock of red disappear into the trees. He gasped, heart fluttering, but crept down the front steps just the same and down the gravel drive, racing as the howl pierced the night just ahead of him.

He crept to the edge of the woods. They were thick here in Alabama back country, and the thicker the woods got, Booger knew, the darker it would get. His flashlight was back in his room, of course, but on the front stoop he hadn't needed it because of the full moon.

Now he cursed himself and inched along the edge of the woods, creeping farther south with each step, toward their new neighbor's house. He could hear the wolf's paws on the dead tree leaves just inside the woods, and every so often he'd see a flash of red.

An ear zipping by, a muscular shoulder or zooming leg, it wasn't just any red, like licorice or candy, but a kind of dark maroon, blood red, and glowing like the harvest moon above.

"Jesus," he muttered to himself, stumbling along over tree roots and the odd rock. "This is too real to be a dream."

The wolf seemed to sense him and ran faster, outpacing Booger as the Franks' home came into view. The lights in the upstairs bedroom were still on and pouring just a little more light onto their yard.

Booger was almost to their street now, and as the trees thinned he crouched near one last trunk, focusing on the street and hoping for a…yes, right there!

For one fleeting moment, there, in the middle of the street, the red wolf stopped. It was clear and bright, glowing in the dark, that rich bloody red fur, fiery eyes red and piercing as they found him clinging to the tree trunk for safety.

It sniffed the air, took one step toward him and then paused, turned her head up toward the moon, opened her long, red snout and howled so loudly Booger thought the moon might come unhinged and tumble from the cloudless sky.

Toni House

Chapter 14

Wizzie got used to Billy working at night. Or, at least, her body did. Now midnight was her new morning, and the time when she could get her chores done and the house spruced up without Billy sticking his stockinged feet all over her just polished coffee table.

She actually kind of liked the weird, almost surreal feeling of brewing a pot of coffee in the middle of the night, turning on all the lights and really going to town to make her new home just right.

She had a job when she met Billy, but he was old-fashioned and preferred her not to work after they got married. But, now he was okay with it if it made her happy, he hated to see her unhappy. The truth be told she kind of missed the comings and goings of her work friends, and it felt isolated being in the big house alone all night, but she was never one to sit idle.

Even if she was sitting, she was doing something productive: knitting or crocheting or sewing or some kind of craft to beautify her home. Sometimes she sold her crafts at local flea markets or donated them to church white sales so she could feel like she was contributing in some way.

But she didn't like to sit until she was right and plum tuckered out from her chores first. And she'd only just gotten started. She took another sip of coffee and winced. She used too much sugar again. Sometimes when she made the coffee after Billy left for another night shift at the plant she was still a little groggy.

But the coffee was strong, and she cranked up the radio. Billy left it on his favorite classic rock station, and she was going to switch it over to country, but then a long guitar solo oozed out and she smiled, leaving it put.

She picked up her bucket full of vinegar and water solution and her squeegee and went to attack the windows. She loved her windows, but only when they were clean.

She set to work, stretching up high on a two-step stool Billy had bought for her nightly chores. She splashed and squeaked and squeegeed her way through all eight of the patio windows, inside and out, and her back and arms were sore by the time she finally dragged her dirty water bucket back inside.

The night was humid, and her bare arms were sweaty even in one of her snug tank tops. *I must look a fright*, she thought, putting her bucket down just inside the kitchen and turning to open the guest bathroom door in the hallway.

There was a full-length mirror on the bathroom side of the door, and she wanted to check just how awful she looked. It was pretty bad, hair mousy and damp, sweat stains on her shirt.

She stood there, in the middle of the night, wired like it was midday, and that's when she saw him: a young Indian brave, behind her in the mirror.

She turned quickly, hand on her pounding chest, but there was nothing there. She blinked twice then turned back to the mirror. He was still there, clear as day.

"Billy," she heard herself say as she stared back at the young brave. He was young, too, older than a teenager but still young, tall and strapping in buckskin pants and a bare torso, arms muscled and wrists bearing a variety of bone or wooden bracelets, or both.

Their eyes met. Wizzie lost herself in those eyes, so young and deep and dark and in such pain. The brave seemed to be trying to tell her something, something important, but never opened his mouth. He reached toward her, long fingers copper-skinned. Only when she felt herself reaching back for him did the reality of what was happening hit her. She screamed and felt her knees go weak.

She slumped to the floor, sweaty forehead against the cold mirror, and fainted.

When she came to, the music was still blaring and the smell of fresh coffee was thick in the air. She was cold inside and out. She glanced at the mirror, almost afraid of what she might see. But it was just her face, blanched and white from shock.

She stood on weak knees and clung to the wall and barstools across from the kitchen counter to peer into the kitchen. The numbers on the stove read 4:38 a.m. She'd been out for nearly an hour.

In all her life, Wizzie had never fainted. Her heartbeat felt weak now, and she shuffled into the kitchen and poured herself a big cup of coffee. She was still ladling in the cream when the front door opened.

"Billy!" she squealed, leaping into his arms. "Thank GOD you're home!"

He chuckled, at first. "What's all this?" he asked, gently prying her from his body. He smelled of snack cakes and fast food but she didn't care. They stood there in the foyer at nearly 5 a.m. but it might as well have been high noon.

"Something just happened," she said, and she caught a slight roll of his eyes.

"Not this again, Baby Dolly," he drawled, sliding into the kitchen to put his lunch pail in the sink. "First the red wolf howling by the mailbox, now…now what happened this time?"

"I saw a brave," she said, pointing to the bathroom door and ignoring his dismissive tone. "A young Indian brave—a young man, really—right there in the guest bathroom mirror."

"Now, Wizzie, I know this job is an adjustment for us both, but —"

"He was as plain to me as you are right now, Billy!" she shouted. "And as close as you are, too."

He heard the tone in her voice and knew better than to ignore her. "And then what happened?" he prodded.

"I…I guess I fainted."

He shook his head and reached out to hug her, but she pushed him away.

"Look in there, Billy," she begged him, turning away. "See if I'm not crazy."

She clung to the kitchen doorframe, listening as he walked heavily in the hallway. She heard the bathroom door open, heard the hinges creak, and listened to the pause as he stared in the mirror.

And waited.

"There's nothing here, Wizzie," he said. "Just a tired and grumpy guy who could use some breakfast."

She turned, rushed to the door and pushed him out of the way. She looked as frantic as ever, hair unruly, tank top dirty, eyes wide with fear. "He was there, Billy, I know he was. I saw him."

"Honey," he said, reaching for her shoulders. She flinched at his touch, a first, and he stood stone-faced as she turned to look at him.

"Don't 'honey' me, Billy Frank. I saw him, and I know what I saw, and nobody, not even you, is going to tell me different."

With that, she clenched her fists and stomped upstairs. There was still dirty water in her pail and a squeegee on the porch, but for once she didn't care. Too wired to sleep, she slipped out onto the widow's walk and paced instead. She was still pacing when Billy crawled into bed and turned all the lights out.

Chapter 15

When Wizzie woke up later that afternoon, Billy had left for work several hours earlier. She made the bed and showered, ready to face the day, or the night, or whatever it was. Wizzie felt both scared and blue, not a great combination for a new wife or homeowner.

Billy and Wizzie had yet to go to bed angry, so this was a first. And so was a howling red wolf by the mailbox in the front yard and a reaching Indian brave in her guest bathroom mirror!

A cup of coffee helped. Wizzie looked on the bathroom mirror for the note Billy usually left her, but it wasn't there. He never let a fight go on this long without leaving her a sweet voice mail or writing her a love note. But she looked far and wide, and found none.

After a third cup of coffee, when she was feeling halfway human, she braved a look inside the guest bathroom mirror. There was nothing except her own reflection.

"Well," she sighed, shutting the bathroom door behind her. "At least I'm clean."

She put her coffee on the foyer table and slipped into the sandals she always left by the door. The day was overcast and gray and she heard the grinding of the school bus's gears as it pulled away from the cul-de-sac.

"Hi, Mrs. Frank," called Booger as she checked the empty mailbox.

"Morning, Booger," she said as he walked over lugging a black and gray backpack.

"Morning?" He laughed, looking weary from his long school day.

She laughed, leaning on the mailbox. "I'm sorry, Booger. Ever since Billy got that new night job at the plastics factory, I'm switched around."

"Yeah." He frowned. "And he never comes fishing with me and Budweiser anymore either."

"Oh, Booger, he will when he gets caught up and life gets back on schedule," she assured the plucky ninth grader.

He nodded, but broke into a yawn, big mouth wide. Wizzie couldn't help herself, she joined him. "Goodness," she said, covering her mouth. "How rude of me."

"You must be sleeping about as good as I am," said Booger.

Wizzie winced at Booger's bad grammar but let it slide. The kid had just gotten off the school bus. He'd had enough learning for one day. "You're not sleeping either?" she asked.

Booger shook his head and looked at his feet. "Can you keep a secret?" he asked.

Wizzie chuckled, wishing she'd brought her cup of coffee along. It was too early in the day for secrets. "Will I be breaking any laws if I say yes?" she asked, only half-jokingly.

"I don't think so," he said, looking up at her.

"I'm joking, Booger. Of course I can keep a secret."

"Well, where you're standing right now..." Booger nodded his head toward the mailbox. "The other night, there was a wolf standing right there, where you are now."

Wizzie stood up straight. "Has Billy been talking to you?" she asked Booger, but by the size of his eyes and the quizzical expression she guessed his answer.

"No-n-no. Why?" he asked, inching closer.

"Because—no, no, I shouldn't. You're frightened enough."

"Because you what?" Booger asked, dropping his backpack to the ground. "You can't leave me hanging now, Mrs. Frank!"

"I-I saw the wolf, too," she confessed, voice low as if the neighbors—what neighbors?—might hear.

"You did?" Booger asked.

Wizzie nodded. "And not only that," she blurted, unable to contain her own secret any longer, "but last night in the bathroom mirror I saw a young Indian brave, clear as day."

"You're sure it was an Indian?" Booger asked, not surprised in the least.

"Yes, with his face painted and leather moccasins," Wizzie assured him.

Booger was pacing now, circling his backpack and muttering. "Do you think they're real?"

Wizzie leaned back against the mailbox, suddenly tired. "They certainly appeared to be real but, an Indian brave in my bathroom? I'm more inclined to believe a wolf in my yard than that."

Booger nodded. "Maybe neither of them are real," he offered, looking up at her. He was getting so tall, she thought to herself. Soon they'd be staring eye to eye. "Have you ever seen *Haunted Happenings*?"

She waved a dismissive hand.

"I'm serious," he said. "This kind of stuff happens all the time. Spirits who can't rest, haunting the last place they took a breath. Maybe—maybe—that is what this is."

She shook her head. "I've never believed in that."

Booger smirked. "That's what everybody on that show says," he assured her. "Until they do…"

Wizzie nodded, and then shook her head. "I dunno, Booger."

He put his hands up as if in surrender. "You don't have to do anything," he promised. "I'll do some digging around on the Internet and see what I come up with."

"Don't tell Billy right now, okay?"

Booger cocked his head and said no more.

"I mean, I-I don't want him to think I'm crazy."

"If we both saw something, Mrs. Frank, you're not crazy."

Chapter 16

The house smelled like cinnamon and pork when Billy walked in at 5 a.m. Strings of white lights, like those you would use at Christmas, hung from several mirrors in the living room and candles flickered on the coffee table.

Soft music played, that jazzy stuff Wizzie liked when she got all romantic-like. He blushed and slid a cardboard box onto the foyer table. "Wizzie?" he called out, slipping his work boots off on the foyer rug like she preferred him to do.

He moped all day after the way they'd fought, and could barely contain himself at work. Two years married and he still hated to leave the house every day, especially when they hadn't spoken all night.

"Honey?" he called again.

He found her sitting on the porch, a glass of wine in her hand, a bottle next to her and a glass on his side of the wicker table between the deck chairs.

"Thank God you're home," she said, leaping into his arms. "It feels like forever since we've talked."

"I know," he said between soft, tender kisses.

"Let's not fight ever again." Wizzie lightly kissed him on the lips.

"Let me see, what are you wearing, Mrs. Frank?"

"Oh, my silky house robe you gave me." She chuckled and pushed him away, pouring his wine.

"Feels a little funny drinking at 5 a.m." He sighed, inching down into the soft cushions she'd made for the Adirondack chairs. "But I like it." The wine was good, nice and dry, the way he liked it.

"It's no different from guys who get home at five and want a hot meal on the stove."

"I'd rather have a hot wife in the kitchen, Baby Dolly."

"Well, if you push it, Billy Boy, you can eat TV dinners again." She slid back into her own chair and pulled her legs up tight. "Or you can have both." She chuckled, voice soft and tight like it got after a glass or two of wine. "I'm sorry we fought, honey."

"Me, too," he said. "It's…you've been so unreasonable with all this wolf nonsense, Wizzie."

He knew before he finished talking that he'd said something stupid.

"I didn't mean to say 'nonsense,'" he said when he saw her look away. "I mean, this is all new to me."

"You don't think it's new to me, Billy Frank?" she said, putting her glass down. "This big old house and you gone half the night?"

"It's what you wanted," he said, sipping his wine. Man, it was good.

"Haven't you ever heard the saying, 'Be careful what you wish for,' Billy?"

He chuckled and poured them both more wine. "It's gonna take a little getting used to for both of us, Wizzie."

She took her glass back and shook her head. "I know what I saw, Billy. You're not gonna tell me different."

Billy nodded, hands up in surrender. Then he smirked. "You didn't turn on all those Christmas lights and light all those candles to fuss at me, did you, Wizzie Frank?"

"Naw," she purred, sliding a hand over to pat his knee. "I made you your favorite, pork roast and cinnamon apples, with cornbread stuffing and pecan pie for dessert."

"Oh Lord," he said, smacking his forehead.

"I thought you loved all that," she said, a worried expression on her face.

"I do," he assured her. "But what are we going to do with all the egg foo yong I picked up at Mr. Fong's All-Night Diner on the way home?"

"You did?" she asked, clutching her chest.

"My peace offering," he explained.

Oh, by the way," She smiles. "I've been hired by the Mitchells down the street to make curtains and a coverlet and redecorate the nursery for their new baby daughter before she's born."

"Hmm, o-okay," Billy stammered. "Wizzie." He held her hand in his, circling the top with his thumb. "It isn't that I don't want you to work—well, I *don't* want you to work—but it's more than that. I'm the man, the husband, the breadwinner. What does it say about me if my wife works, that I can't provide for her needs and wants? So if you really want to work, fine, work but I don't want you to think you have to. Wizzie I love you and all I want is for you to be happy."

"Billy, I love that you want to give me everything, but I've always worked and I love making my own money and that I am contributing in some way." She smiled and put down her wineglass. "I have an idea," she said, reaching for his hand as she slid from her chair and straddled his lap.

"Oh, Mrs. Frank, I see you have nothing underneath that silky robe."

"Let's go upstairs and make up, and we can decide on what we want to eat after."

He smiled, soft and lazy. "Or maybe we can get so hungry we'll want to eat it all."

She chuckled, warm and happy, just the way he liked. "That sounds like a plan, Billy Frank."

Chapter 17

"What'd you do?" Billy asked, cracking open a soda and sitting back in his chair. "Take the week off from school to put all this together?"

Booger grinned nervously. "I probably should have," he said, stifling his yawn. "My history teacher, Mr. Conlon, would probably have given me extra credit."

Booger reached for his own soda and stood next to the poster board "map" he'd prepared. As Wizzie and Billy sat on their cushioned deck chairs, in front of them sat a printout with a few pages of history Booger had dug up during his online search of the ghosts that had been haunting him and Wizzie all week.

He cleared his throat and began his presentation. "Thanks, you guys, for agreeing to listen to me," he began, watching Wizzie smile and Billy roll his eyes. That was okay; Booger was used to folks rolling their eyes at him.

"First, you can read the papers in front of you later because I'll tell you what they say right now."

Wizzie nodded her encouragement, a glass of iced tea sweating onto the coaster beside her.

"Basically, our street, Deer Run Ridge, sits on what used to be prime Mecklesh Indian land."

Billy shifted in his seat but Booger noticed he perked up a bit, giving him the confidence to go on. He turned to his map, which took him two straight nights—and plenty of smears, smudges and false starts—to get right.

"Here is Wolf Creek." He pointed out a blue line of "water" that ran along most of his map. "Here is my house," he said, pointing to a purple square along the creek, "and here is yours." Booger pointed to a red square for the Franks' house.

"And this circle," he said, moving his hand in a circular motion around Deer Run Ridge, "is where the Mecklesh Indians buried their people."

Billy sat back in his chair. "You're telling me we're living on an old Indian burial ground," he scoffed. "Haven't there been enough horror movies about that very thing, Booger?"

Booger smiled; the man knew his late-night monster TV. "Yes, there have, but that doesn't change the fact that our government basically bullied the Mecklesh Tribe off their land in the 1830s."

He looked at the map and smiled. It really was pretty good. Then he cleared his throat and pointed to the creek. "Many battles were fought alongside Wolf Creek. In fact, for a time, the chief of the Mecklesh Tribe renamed the body of water the River of Blood. It was horrible. The white man and the Indians fought and the people died. Legend says the water was the color of blood and the stench of death didn't leave for fifty years."

Booger slid a printout from behind the map and walked closer to his audience of two. "This is him," he said, looking at the old black and white photo he found on a history site about the state of Alabama.

"His name was Chief Running Blood, and he was one of the best hunters in all the southern tribes."

Booger handed the picture to Wizzie, who winced when she saw it. Booger couldn't blame her. The man in the picture was both noble and savage, with fine, ancient features but cold, dead eyes. He wore a permanent scowl, it seemed, and in his ornate headdress and elaborate war paint would have been right at home in an old black and white western movie.

"Then how come I've never heard of him?" Billy teased.

Booger shrugged. "I guess history only has room for a few big names, like Sitting Bull or Pocahontas, but the man was real, and the white men feared him. The Mecklesh Tribe was part of the mighty Creek Nation that ran through most of the South including Georgia and Alabama. But he fought with everyone, his own people, with our people, the governments, the Army, even with General Bradley hear tell, that General Bradley tried to keep the peace but the chief would have none of it, and at the end no one would stand by or with him."

Billy nodded, finally impressed as he stared at Chief Running Blood's picture.

"Finally, the chief proclaimed death to all white people, not just the soldiers who tried to take his people's land but anyone with white skin, farmers, shopkeepers, wives and even children. Forever. The legend also says that there was something more, a deeper hate for the white man than just them taking his land. It was more about bloodline, about being pure. I couldn't find any more information about the bloodline."

The porch grew quiet, the lazy Saturday afternoon stretching out as far as the eye could see on what had once been thriving Native American soil.

"Finally," Booger concluded, "his own people could take no more of their chief's violence. His tribe began to dwindle until at last all that remained were a few young braves as crazy as their chief or perhaps just young enough to have fallen under his spell. Finally, even they turned on him. Legend has it that one young warrior, a brave named Red Wolf, challenged Chief Running Blood to end his reign of violence. But he remained defiant to the end..."

Booger's voice trailed off, causing Billy to prompt him. "How?" he asked. "How was Chief Running Blood defiant to the end?"

Booger looked up from his display board and peered at the curious couple. "Apparently, as Red Wolf and Chief Running Blood fought to their deaths, the angry chief vowed his revenge on all who had wronged him."

Booger slumped into the chair next to him, exhausted from the long week of preparing all that he had learned. Wizzie got up and handed him a soda and a candy bar from the refreshments she'd brought onto the porch.

"That's a lot of work you did there," she said, sitting back down as he guzzled the soda before chowing down on the candy bar. "Is it all true?"

Booger looked back at her and nodded. "I double- and triple-checked all my sources," he said, the sugar and caffeine reviving him. He didn't think he'd slept more than five hours a night since he'd started his little research project.

"Where?" Billy asked, standing up and pacing the length of the porch. As he passed in front of Booger's "map," he pointed to the blue marker that represented Wolf Creek. "Where did this Red Wolf brave fight to the death with Chief Running Blood?"

Booger leaned over and pointed farther up the map, past their red and purple houses. "Dead Man's Cliff is just up here, at the base of that little finger of the Alabama River that feeds into Wolf Creek."

Billy followed a short dotted line back to their cul-de-sac. "So why did they bury their people all the way back here?" he asked.

"That whole map was theirs," Booger pointed out, "and about a hundred more miles of prime Alabama coastline that wouldn't fit on my sheet of poster board. I guess, to them, a day's walk wasn't too far to bury their dead."

Billy nodded, studying the map. The sky had darkened now, dusk blending into early evening as Booger slumped in his chair. Porch lights grew brighter as the darkness encroached.

Wizzie stood, too, and kind of leaned into Billy. Booger smiled as Billy automatically slid his arm, long and lazy, over her shoulder. "Booger, why was the young brave who fought his chief to the death named Red Wolf?"

Booger smiled. "Another legend has it that one young brave found a wolf pup in the wild. The Mecklesh tribe had killed its mother during a hunt, and the rest of the braves were going to abandon it. He couldn't, or wouldn't, and raised it as a pet. The wolf grew to be a fierce and worthy warrior of its own, and had a distinguishing hide of blood-red fur. So they changed the brave's name to Red Wolf, and called the wolf Tala."

"Why?" Wizzie pressed. "Why 'Tala,' Booger?"

Booger shrugged. "As far as I could tell, in some Native American language 'Tala' was their word for red wolf, or stalking wolf, or big wolf or fierce wolf. So it fit, I guess."

Suddenly, Billy tensed, gently shoving Wizzie away so he could look down at her, and then over at Booger. "Hold up, now," he began, talking with his hands as he paced some more. "So this is all you think…Wizzie, is this about that durn wolf you keep telling me about?"

Wizzie looked at Booger almost sadly, then back at her husband. "Of course it is, Billy. Why do you think Booger agreed to put on this whole show for us? He's…he's seen it, too, haven't you, Booger?"

Booger nodded. "Every few nights, Mr. Frank, the big red wolf howls in the street. I'm surprised you haven't heard it yourself."

And then, as if on cue, there came a sound, low and gentle at first, as if perhaps it was just a breeze. They all stopped right where they were, pricking up their ears. Then the sound grew, harder and harder to deny.

At last the howling rose to a crescendo. "What in tarnation?" asked Billy.

"That's it!" said Wizzie, tugging on Billy's sleeve. "That's what we've been talking about!"

"Let's go see," said Booger, but before he could take two steps the howling stopped. It was replaced by the slow crunching of dead leaves as something large approached them.

"Look," said Billy, voice catching, as he pointed off the porch. There, on the banks of Wolf Creek, the red wolf stood, peering at them all with blazing red eyes.

Billy inched forward, hand raised slightly, and the wolf darted out of sight. Not with loud footsteps or a long gait, but as if it had simply vanished into the early evening misty fog.

Chapter 18

"Thanks for taking the time to see me, Mr. McLellan."

"Please, call me Matt," Billy's boss said as they settled across from each other in the break room of Peterson's Plastics. Matt had a vending machine cup of coffee and a sleeve of white powdered donuts in front of him.

Billy had a warm can of soda from home, but had barely touched it.

"What's going on, Billy?" Matt asked, white powder dusted across his thick lips.

It was two in the morning and there were still another two hours to go before his shift as night watchman ended. He was nervous and antsy after Booger's "presentation" on the porch the night before.

"I know I'm new here but..." Billy paused. He didn't want to risk his job, but it killed him that Wizzie was home alone with some "ghost wolf" prowling around the neighborhood at night. "Is there any way I can catch the next shift?"

Matt arched an eyebrow. "From four to noon?" he asked, as if Billy was joking. "That's prime territory, Billy, you know that."

"I know, I mean, I'm willing to take a dock in pay or whatever. I just…I really need to be home at night."

Matt polished off two more powdered donuts in quick succession before shaking his head. "You never indicated there would be a problem when you applied, Billy."

Billy nodded. "There wasn't, there isn't, a problem, I just…my wife gets a little jumpy in the new house at night, you know?" No way was Billy explaining to his new boss, or any other grown man, that his new house was haunted by the ghost of an angry, homicidal Indian chief.

"Mine, too, brother, but here I am, doing inventory once a month just the same. And I'm a manager, right, so…the man who has the four to noon shift has been with Peterson's for fourteen years, Billy. And he's a good man, a happy man, so I don't think he'll be switching shifts with you anytime soon."

Billy nodded, sitting back in the plastic molded chair. "I know it's a lot to ask, Matt," he said as his new boss finished off his donuts and washed them down with the last of his coffee. "But I wouldn't be bugging you if it wasn't important."

Matt crinkled up his donut wrapper and slid it inside his empty Styrofoam cup. "What's so important, Billy?" he asked impatiently. "I mean, I can't help you if I don't know what the problem is."

Billy sat there, mind reeling with what to say. *I really should have thought this out first before asking to see him,* he thought to himself. Meanwhile, Matt fidgeted, barely disguising several glances at the cheap wristwatch on his beefy arm.

"Is it marital troubles?" he asked almost eagerly, as if he hoped it might be. "The little wife not trusting you out on the town at all hours?"

"No," Billy snapped. Then, a little softer, he added, "No, not at all, nothing like that. It's just…she's going through some things and hasn't been sleeping well."

Matt stood briskly, as if disappointed. "Know what I do when I don't sleep well, Billy?" He shoved his chair in roughly and reached into the front pocket of his polyester slacks. "I take a sleeping pill. Here's a couple bucks, buy her some on the way home after your shift is over. In two hours," he called out over his shoulder, crossing the deserted break room in six easy strides.

Billy stood, too, leaving crumpled bills on the table and sliding his uniform hat from beside them. He said nothing as he left the room, pausing by the door to text Wizzie at home.

"No deal," he wrote plainly, turning off the phone so he wouldn't have to read the disappointment in his wife's follow-up texts.

Toni House

Chapter 19

Wizzie woke from a dead sleep with every light in the house on. She blinked from the intensity of the glare from the table lamp next to her and looked at her watch. It read 3:08 a.m.

Another hour or so before Billy got home. She rose groggily, surprised that she'd fallen asleep in the middle of her chores. The dusting rag was on the coffee table in front of her, next to a fresh can of Shine Away furniture polish.

The radio was still on, crooning an old George Jones song, one she never much cared for. She turned it off on the way into the kitchen, shaking her head.

One minute she'd been high as a kite, three cups of coffee into the first few hours of the new day, whiling away the hours until Billy came home. She'd washed windows and switched out a load of laundry and dusted when, boom, she crashed.

She sat down for a minute, to rest her eyes…over an hour ago. Now she tossed out the old coffee grounds and brewed a new pot, nibbling on a leftover piece of coffee cake from a wedge in tinfoil in the fridge.

She checked her reflection in the microwave. Her long hair was askew, half of her bright red cleaning bandana dangling over one eye. She straightened herself, fixed her cup of coffee and leaned against the kitchen counter to let it cool.

The groaning began at 3:17 a.m. She knew because she was glancing at the digital readout on the microwave when she first heard it. Low, cold and masculine, it wasn't coming from outside the open screen doors of the patio, but from inside the house.

She stood stock-still, steaming coffee halfway to her lips, then without warning the power cut off. The glowing blue numbers on the microwave clock dimmed and disappeared.

The air conditioning was still on, humming in the darkness. But then it whined to a stop, leaving the house in an eerie, dark silence. Hands trembling, she set the coffee down, suddenly as awake as if it was Sunday at noon.

The groaning resumed. Her eyes squeezed shut as her hands found each other, clenching to keep them from shaking. "Sweet Jesus," she muttered, half a prayer, half a curse. "Lord God Almighty, when will this nightmare end?"

As if in response to her muttering, the groaning increased, the very floor under her feet beginning to shake. She shrank deeper into the kitchen, farther from the groaning noise, but even pressed tight against the oven the voice grew louder, as if to follow her, pursue her.

She unclenched her eyes at last, finding the hallway beyond the kitchen illuminated by a faint, rosy light. It seemed to draw her near, despite her paralyzing fear.

She inched toward the hallway, touching the cold stove and the kitchen counter as she crawled forward, as if for security. She clutched at the kitchen doorway, clean white wood under her white knuckles.

Now that she was closer to its source, she could see a light growing brighter, redder, down the hall. She inched closer still, one hand on the wall as if she took it away, she might be pulled down the hall, faster, faster, and sucked away into the glowing red light.

It seemed to be coming from around the corner, in the little alcove under the stairs where Wizzie and Billy shared their tiny workspace; he with his fishing lures and fantasy football statistics, she with her patterns and sewing machine and stacks of fabric lining every available surface.

Closer she crept, closer and closer, until the light grew brighter. It flowed from within the room, oozing like fog through the cracks around, above and below the door.

She could go no further. Wizzie stopped, facing the door, midway between the kitchen and around the corner from the living room. The groaning grew louder, and she began to hear it was more than indistinct moans or sounds, but instead a word being repeated over and over again.

"*Ele,*" came the groan, more persistent now, clearer. It was forceful and dramatic, an old sound, like something from a western movie. The voice...the voice of a brave Indian chief. "Ele."

It sounded like the way people said "LA" for Los Angeles, only with an emphasis on the "A" sound: El...lay.

"*El...lay.*"

She shook her head, fists clenched at her side, shoulders pressed tight against the wall at her back, stifling a scream.

As if to make her shock complete, the glow around the door grew brighter, and the voice became even louder and more insistent.

"*El...lay. El...lay. El...lay.*"

She whimpered, low and soft, when all of a sudden keys—real, live keys—turned in the front door lock.

"Billy!" she gasped, turning and rushing toward the foyer.

The front door opened and, as if on cue, the groaning stopped, the glow darkened to pitch black and faded away, and the lights flickered on. Suddenly the entire house was bathed in light and her white knight, Billy, was standing there, shielding his eyes from the glow.

"I'm gonna have to get a second job just to pay the light bill, woman," he teased, putting his lunch box down. "I came home early on account I knew you get so lonely." He smoothed her hair, his heart pounding to match the beats of her own. "Wizzie, darlin', what's wrong?"

"You need to call that realtor woman," she spat, pushing him away and yanking off her red kerchief. She shoved it in a back pocket and finger-combed her hair. "I want to know who had this house before us, and what in tarnation he did to tick off the whole Indian Nation!"

Chapter 20

"Carol?" Billy asked, pacing the hardwood floor of the patio as he finally got through to the realtor's number. "Carol Washburn?"

"Yes," came a voice, practically yawning.

"Carol, it's Billy Frank, from the place out on Wolf Creek?"

The voice on the other end of the line grew cautious, almost cold. "Billy, for Pete's sake, it's seven in the morning."

Billy shook his head. "Carol, trust me, I know exactly what durn time it is because I've been pacing the floorboards of my durn porch for the last three hours, waiting for it to be daylight so I could call at a proper hour."

"Well, I'd prefer you call back during business hours, *Mr*. Frank. As it is I only came into the office for a moment on my way out to an appointment on Sunburn Road, so—"

"And I'd appreciate you telling me just who owned this house before us, *Mrs*. Washburn."

There was a long pause on the other end of the line, so long Billy thought she might have hung up. Finally, he heard a dry cough. "I'm afraid I can't share that information with you, Billy."

He smirked. So it was "Billy" again now, huh? "Well, Carol," he replied, "I know I can look it up in County Records, but they don't open until nine and I'd rather hear it from the horse's mouth, if you don't mind."

The fact was, he already pulled the records from the county website and had them, printed and still warm, in his hot little hands. But she didn't need to know that.

"If you're having second thoughts about the place, Billy..." she mumbled.

"Whatever makes you think that?" he snapped. "The fact that I've been up all night consoling my poor wife, who hasn't had a good night's sleep since we moved in, maybe? Or the fact that I can't leave her alone for a simple eight-hour shift at the plastics plant without hearing some new ghost story when I get home? Or the fact that I'm yelling into the phone on a Tuesday morning at 7 a.m.?"

He could feel his cheeks blushing red and ears aflame as his voice echoed in the new light of day. He counted to ten, spun in a circle at the far end of the porch, and hustled back in the other direction.

"I'd appreciate it if you'd calm down a bit, Billy. I'm not sure how I, as your former realtor, can help you—"

Billy guffawed, openly and loudly. "So it's 'former' realtor now, is it? So soon, Carol?"

Her voice came back, swift and stiff. "Well, you understand you've lived in the house long enough that the contract is firm. That means to move out you'd have to sell the house, and—"

"I'm well aware of the terms of our contract, Carol," Billy spat, noting the voluminous file folder marked "realtor" sitting on the porch coffee table, wrinkled and unfolded from Billy's morning reading. "And I can move out any time I wish if that's my desire.

What I'm asking you, point blank, before I call your boss and tell him what kind of scam you're pulling, is who lived here before me, for how long and why they left. I don't think that's asking too much, now, is it, Carol?"

"I'm not sure how calling my boss is going to make you feel any better," Carol said, a bit more cautious now. "But if you must know, the previous tenants were another young couple, much like yourself. As you know, you got a great price on a very large plot of land and a remodeled home done to the nines. That's because, frankly, said young couple were a little skittish."

"Skittish?" he barked. "Could you remind me which they were more skittish about, Carol? The fact that their home was built on sacred Indian ground or because of the glowing red wolf that haunted their mailbox or the glowing red lights from under the stairs or the constant moaning, clacking and—"

"Billy, if you'll just calm down we can talk about this like adults. Why don't you come into my office later this week? We can—"

"We can what, Carol?" Billy huffed, staring at the printout from the county website. "Will we talk about the Tanners? That's the name of the young couple who lived here before us, right? You said they cut out after 'awhile.' Says here in the county records they bolted after less than a month. After that, the house sat vacant for two years before you could unload it on us. And before the Tanners were the Carmichaels. They lived here for a whole six weeks before they bolted, and before that it was the Frasiers, the Phillipses and the Shaws. None stayed for more than a year, and this goes back decades. In fact, I'd say this house has been vacant longer than it's been lived in."

He paused, out of breath, tossing the crinkled printout onto one of Wizzie's lovingly stitched seat cushions.

"I can neither confirm nor deny all of those residents, Billy, but clearly you've done your homework. Now if we can just talk—"

Billy heard a scream from inside the house and dropped the phone at once. Carol was still squawking—"Billy, is that you? Billy, are you still there?"—as he almost ran through the screen door before he whipped it open and ran inside.

Wizzie stood at the bottom of the stairs just inside the doorway to their little office. Her slack face was as white as the wall to which she clung and she was shaking, obviously petrified.

"What's wrong?" he asked, approaching her slowly as one might a sleepwalker. She seemed dazed, eyes half open, skin clammy. "Wizzie? Honey?"

At last she looked at him, blinking twice before her eyes seemed to focus. "You!" she said, pointing at him with a trembling finger. "You brought that in here, didn't you, Billy?"

Billy was tired, strung out, and fearful. "Brought what?" he snapped, looking beyond her and into the room. "What did I bring…" His voice faded as he saw the open cooler, river water still briny and yellow in the bottom, and the old bone he'd found in Wolf Creek sticking up out of the top.

He'd meant to come in and retrieve the cooler, dry out the bone, and study it more carefully, maybe even snap a few pictures with his digital camera and share them online to see what folks in some archeology forums might think.

Instead, between the new job and Wizzie's seemingly nightly hauntings, he'd simply forgotten.

"How could you?" she gasped, her mouth still open and hand clinging to the wall as he stood in the doorway of the small office space. "How could you bring that into our home?"

"How did you find it?" he asked, half embarrassed, half amazed. Wizzie could barely change a coffee filter, let alone an air filter, and he'd fastened the vent so tightly.

She ran away from him up the stairs, hovering between the hallway and the vast expanse of the living room filling up with morning light. "I wanted to see, now that you were home, if there was a rational explanation for the red glow I saw in that room." Her voice was tight as she avoided his eyes. "I thought maybe you'd left a movie on your laptop, or I'd left a device on and the battery light was glowing, but nothing in there was on. And then I saw some rust on the floor beneath the air vent, and I went to clean it up and…and…one of the screws was loose, something was glowing from back there, so…"

Billy filled in the rest of the details for himself. "I'm sorry," he said, inching forward, but she only shrank back from him, a first. "I was going to clean it up and study it."

"Where did it come from?" she asked, finally looking up at him, eyes wide in horror. "Where on earth did you find it?"

"I was fishing with Booger in Wolf Creek," he admitted. "My lure snagged on it and I dragged it from the water."

"Why didn't you tell me?" she asked, voice catching. She sounded hurt, sad, and betrayed.

"I was going to tell you once I had it all nice and cleaned up and figured out where it came from."

Wizzie shook her head. "So until then you kept it in a cooler and hid it in the air vent?"

He blushed. "Sounds stupid now, but I had good intentions."

She seemed to snap out of it then, fear and anxiety and judgment flying out the window and the old Wizzie, the housekeeper extraordinaire, came back into her eyes. "*Billy Frank*, I want that bone *OUT* of this house at once." She stood, face stern, arm extended, finger pointed at the front door. *"Now."*

"But, Wizzie," he protested, peering down at the round nub of the bone poking out of the cooler. "I haven't even started cleaning it—"

"Billy, you didn't see it but last night, shoot, four hours ago there was a red light as bright as your ball cap glowing from this very room, and a groaning, a groaning like you've never heard. You think it's a coincidence all that happened in the very room you hid a human leg *bone*?"

She was red-faced and almost shrieking again, and he put out a hand to reassure her but she slapped it away.

"Out, now! Take it out where you found it and bury it again. Right now," she screamed, pointing to the door again.

"I'm not going to—"

She waved him away. "When did you say you found that bone again?"

He hung his head. "I didn't, Wizzie."

She frowned. "Was it that first time you and Booger went fishing? Wasn't that three, four weeks ago? Just after we moved in?" She was pacing, walking in a tight circle around an ottoman she'd been reupholstering all week.

"Billy?" Her voice was high and tight as she turned, biting on a nail. "Don't you see? That's right when these hauntings started!"

Chapter 21

"I don't know, Mr. Frank," Booger said, turning his *Haunted Happenings* hat around on his forehead. "Mrs. Frank has a point. I mean, I started seeing the red wolf about three weeks ago, too, so…"

"Don't you go starting in on me, too," Billy sassed, dumping a shovelful of dirt at his feet.

Booger dodged it just in time. It smelled like sulfur, but nowhere near as bad as the bone. It reeked of river water, death and decay.

"I can't believe neither of you smelled this," Booger said, waving a hand in front of his nose as he knelt down to look at the bone more closely.

It was still moist, and dirty like the river it came from. "Thing is," Billy said between digging up a long, deep hole on the riverbank, "it was fine until I brought it out of the house. It only started smelling just this morning."

Booger looked up, nodding. "Maybe the bone doesn't want to be buried," he said.

"Now, Booger," Billy said, taking a break and resting one arm on his shovel while dragging the other across his sweaty forehead. Even the long bill of his trusty red ball cap couldn't keep the noonday sun out of Billy's eyes.

Booger remained crouched by the bone and sniffed it gently. He winced and held his hands up in defeat. "I'm just saying, if this bone really is what's causing your house and front yard to be haunted, don't you think it has the power to fight back when you're trying to bury the curse?"

"By smelling like an old gym sock that's been soaked in dead fish excrement?" Billy joked.

Booger frowned, standing, and inched away from the open beer cooler. "An old gym sock filled with a dead, rotten possum, with skunk for good measure," he corrected.

Billy snorted, reaching down into a second cooler, this one blue and filled with ice. He took a swig from his second beer of the morning.

Booger was out of school for the day, thanks to a teacher in-service at Jefferson High School. He stumbled on Mr. Frank when he was going out fishing, and quickly locked Budweiser in the garage, much to the poor dog's dismay—an old smelly bone in a gross red cooler, come on!—and traded his fishing pole for his favorite book on ghosts.

He picked up the book he brought along with him, something thick and black called *Life After Haunting: How to Bury the Dead, Once and For All*. He was on page 378 when he settled in on the rock on the shore of Wolf Creek and began reading out loud:

> " *'Ghosts walk the earth, unsettled creatures unable, or*
>
> *unwilling, to relinquish their anger, fear or dismay. They are*
> *confused, or convinced, that their life is not over, or that it is*
> *somehow unfinished. Hauntings happen when others,*
> *humans, interfere with a ghost's mission, or invade their*

space. If, by chance, one happens to obtain a physical piece of the human that became a ghost, such as a lock of hair from an old comb, a fingernail or perhaps a bone fragment or full bone, burying it should cease all evidence of haunting forever… "'

Billy stood silently, face grim in the noonday sun. "There you have it then," he said, nodding, and returned to his makeshift shallow grave. "We bury the bone, we stop the haunting, Wizzie gets some sleep, and I can go to work without her texting me a hundred times a shift. We all win."

Booger put the book down and frowned. "It said 'should cease all evidence of a haunting,' Mr. Frank. That's no guarantee."

Billy tossed another mound of wet dirt at his feet and this time Booger was too slow to get out of the way. It landed, ripe and pungent, on the toe of his old black sneakers. He kicked it off and dragged his shoes through the high river grass a few times for good measure.

"I asked for your help," Billy said, nodding toward the open cooler, "not your opinion. Now, bring me that bone."

"M-m-me?" Booger stammered, backing away with his hands up. "Why me?"

Billy leaned on his shovel again and nodded toward the big black book on the mossy rock. "You're the ghost expert, aren't you?"

Booger shook his head, even as he approached the bone sticking out of the cooler.

"Besides," Billy teased, "if I tell Wizzie I grabbed that bone with my own hands, she'd never let me touch her again."

"Very funny," croaked Booger as he dragged the cooler toward the grave. It was long and low, about three feet deep. "Do you think that's deep enough?"

"Quit stalling," Billy urged, leaning on his shovel and watching Booger curiously. "I figured you'd be all over this, a kid who watches as many ghost shows as you."

"TV is one thing," Booger said absently, "this is another." But still, Mr. Frank was right: how could he watch every ghost story known to man and not want to be a part of one unraveling in his own backyard? Literally in his own backyard?

He nodded and grabbed the bone. It was wet and unnaturally cold. He looked up, only to find Billy finishing his beer. Booger quickly slid the bone inside the hole. It lay there, harmless looking, but still Booger's fingers felt cold as ice.

"Here," he said, yanking the wooden part of the shovel out from under Billy's hand and piercing the mound of soil with its blade. "Let me finish."

Quickly, Booger filled in the hole. He was breathing heavy, sweating, arms like pistons back and forth, the sound of wet, sloshing mud filling his ears as sweat stung his eyes, but he didn't stop until the hole was filled, and then some.

"Hey, hey, kid," Mr. Frank said quietly, softly, gently pressing his shoulder. "Booger, man, it's okay, you're done."

And still Booger shrugged him off, digging out dirt from around the grave and piling it on top, higher, higher, until it was more mound than a level stretch of land.

"Okay, now, Booger, okay…" Billy crooned.

Finally spent, Booger handed him the shovel. He stumbled back from the grave, the mound, until he sat on the mossy rock. He looked down, arms muddy, shirt drenched in sweat, hands stinging. When he turned them over, he saw why: his palms were bloody from the shovel and what he'd done with it.

Funny, he thought, he hadn't felt a thing.

Chapter 22

Wizzie heard the grass crunching from half a mile away, but she wasn't afraid; she knew it was no ghost. That's because Booger began calling out to her, "Mrs. Frank, Mrs. Frank, do NOT be scared. It's just me, Booger…" over and over again.

Finally, before someone called the cops, she had to stand at the porch railing and hiss, "Okay, Booger, I get it; you're not a haunted wolf! Now, get up here before you wake the whole neighborhood."

Booger ran across the backyard, a flashlight in his hand sending a bobbling beam of light up and down the banks of Wolf Creek.

"Sorry." He huffed and puffed, a hand on each knee as he stood at the bottom of the porch steps trying—and failing—to catch his breath. "I just…didn't…want you…to be…scared," he gasped.

She smiled and poured him a glass of lemonade. It was Saturday night, well, almost Sunday morning, and Billy had gone in to work. "What are you doing out this late?" she asked as he slithered up the porch steps and into the wicker chair facing her. "Does your mother know you're over here? She'll tan your hide when she finds out, and I'm not one for aiding and abetting fugitives, let me tell you."

She was both wagging a finger and wearing a smile. The fact was, she was relieved to see Booger—to see anyone—instead of sitting alone peering into the dark, waiting for a glowing red wolf, or worse, to creep up on her.

Booger shook his head. "Not even Budweiser knows I snuck out, Wizzie."

Wizzie cocked an eyebrow as Booger used her first name, but she had to admit hearing him call her "Mrs. Frank" all the time made her feel kind of old.

"Still," she said, "it's not safe being out here so late, Booger. You could have tripped over a rock or a tree limb and hit your head and fallen in the river and…well…"

She shivered at the thought.

He did, too, sipping greedily at his lemonade. She watched his eyes flit around the porch and then wander inside, through the sliding glass doors and into the living room.

She followed them, seeing what he saw: all the lights on, candles flickering all over the porch. It might have been high noon for how bright it was inside and out—and that's exactly how she liked it.

Their eyes met, both flicking away quickly as if embarrassed. She busied herself pouring him another glass of lemonade until he said, "Where's Billy? Uh, I mean…Mr. Frank?"

"He's at work, sugar," she said, leaning back into her chair.

He nodded as if suddenly understanding. A small smirk slid across his face, cheeks still pink from running across the lawn. "So that's why this place is lit up brighter than a Christmas tree!"

She nodded, blushing by candlelight. "Can you blame me, Booger, with all that's been going on lately?"

He shook his head eagerly. "You should see my room. Mom says she's gonna take back half my allowance when the light bill comes in!"

They laughed nervously, loudly, as if to beat back the night. But when at last the laughter subsided, there was nothing but the sound of the night to greet them.

"Don't think I'm not grateful for the company, Booger, but why'd you come over here at almost midnight on a Saturday night?"

His face fell, looking grim. "Well, you know how the other day you told me about that word you kept hearing in the hallway?"

Wizzie felt a chill. "*El...lay.*" She shivered as she repeated it, eyes looking past Booger into the darkness that surrounded Wolf Creek. "*El...lay.*"

He nodded, creeping forward in his seat. "Well, I went on the Internet and have been looking around and found out it's not just a sound, but a word. It comes from the old Creek Nation, an assembly of Indian tribes from around this area, and it means foot, or leg, depending which site you use to translate it."

She shook her head, though she certainly believed him. She just couldn't believe all of this was happening.

"And I figured, with the leg you made Billy, er, Mr. Frank, bury...maybe somehow the two were connected."

"Of course they're connected!" she snapped, suddenly regretting it. Booger's face fell again, and she reached out to touch his knee. "I mean, well, don't you think?" Her tone was softer this time.

He chuckled. "Why do you think I'm here instead of back home in bed, watching a *Haunted Happenings* marathon?"

They both chuckled again. He sighed, standing.

"So what now?" Wizzie asked, standing to join him. He seemed to be growing so fast; they were nearly the same height.

He smiled, a little bashful. "Well," he began, "I guess…I guess I just wanted you to know it's over. I mean, whatever voice you heard, whoever's voice you heard, it was saying 'foot' or 'leg' and, well, I suppose you know your husband and I buried the only leg around, so —"

He suddenly stopped speaking, and it was no surprise why. In the distance, low and soft, came a growl. It was unmistakable, and their eyes met, wide and sad.

"You were saying?" Wizzie moaned, slumping back into her chair and slapping her forehead.

Booger looked

left, then right. The wolf's howl seemed to come from both directions, and neither, at once. "I thought…" he mumbled, turning toward her, voice cracking as if he'd just that moment reached puberty. "I thought it was over."

Chapter 23

Billy looked at the cell phone resting in the cup holder of his pickup truck, surprised to see no new text messages from Wizzie. It was nearly 4:30 a.m. and he hadn't heard from her since before his shift.

Usually she texted him a couple of times an hour to check in or say "Hi" or text a long row of X's and O's telling him she was sending him hugs and kisses.

He knew she got lonely wandering around the old house, especially after her chores were done and she relaxed to listen to music or watch TV while waiting for him to walk through the door.

It was that last hour or two, she said, that made her realize she was alone, standing, sitting, pacing, staring at the door, until she gave up, zonked out, or read one of her mushy love stories.

But he smiled as he turned off the main strip of darkened fast food restaurants and neon-lit gas stations, heading for home. Ever since he'd buried that bone near the river, the hauntings had stopped and all had been quiet.

Sure, only a couple of days had passed so far, but those forty-eight hours had been sheer bliss, mainly for Wizzie. She'd been sleeping better, eating better and, luckily for him, kissing him more than snapping at him.

The windows were open, the fall air cool against his bare arm as he drove, off a little early for the third night in a row. It was slow at the plant, and Billy hoped they wouldn't lay him off so soon after hiring him. He had a wife to support, and a new mortgage payment to boot.

Still, he wasn't too worried. Now that he'd quit asking for every other night off to hold Wizzie's hand, his boss at the plant, Matt, had been pretty cool. He didn't think Matt would be letting him go anytime soon. And even if he did, Billy figured there were plenty of other plants around that might need a young, steady, experienced night watchman.

All in all, Billy Frank was feeling pretty good as he drove home that night. He passed the general store that marked the turnoff for his street and sat up a little straighter as he neared the house. He could see lights on in the distance, the porch light growing bright and steering him home.

And that's when the howl rumbled through the open windows, making the hair on his arms stand up and forcing him to slam on the brakes. There, in the middle of the road, stood a wolf. It was as tall as the hood of his truck, and nearly as red.

"Holy…" Billy whispered, voice tight with emotion, namely fear, but he never finished the curse. He sat, the engine idling, the wolf meeting his eyes as Billy stared out through the dirty windshield.

The wolf opened her mouth to howl, but only whined a little, curiously, beseechingly, as if she wanted—as if she expected—something from Billy.

Billy left the engine running and quietly cracked open the door as if afraid to spook the wolf. But the wolf stood, watching his every move, eyes a brilliant, glowing red, redder than the rest of her, which was saying something.

They stood facing each other, Billy waiting for the giant beast to bolt with every step he took. And he took them, one after the other, hardly believing this was happening.

The closer he got, the bigger the wolf seemed. She glowed, as if her coat of slick, glossy fur was on fire, as if she might radiate a great, pulsing heat, but just the opposite was true. With each step, the surrounding air grew colder, until at last Billy was shivering.

He reached out a hand tentatively, inching closer, waiting for the wolf to growl, or run, or even bite. But she just stood, staring with those intense red eyes, until Billy was close enough and brave enough to stroke her fur.

Only there was no fur. His hand landed in mist, cold and fiery at the same time. The glowing wolf evaporated into red fog as Billy touched it. Billy stood there, looking stupid, his arm petting nothing, his throat dry and his heart pounding.

He stood there for the longest time, staring where the wolf had been. He didn't know whether to be relieved that his wife wasn't crazy or disappointed that the wolf wasn't real. For either way, something ghastly was happening to their home, and whatever he'd done—or thought he'd done—with the bone hadn't worked.

He turned and dropped his head, tired and defeated, but stopped mid-stride. There in the dirt, thick and deep, were four paw prints. He knelt, putting his hand in one, where it was fairly swallowed by the deep, wide, unmistakable print of a giant wolf.

The print was cold but fresh, crisp and clear in the rich, loamy dirt that surrounded their property. He stood at last, shivering, and shuffled back to his truck. He slid onto the seat, put it in drive and purposefully angled his truck to steer straight over the prints.

He sighed, relieved, as the front door came into view. He was wondering whether to tell Wizzie when she opened the door and crept onto the top step, holding the screen door open. She was putting on a brave face, but he saw the mascara smeared under one eye—she must have missed it.

"Did you hear it?" she asked, taking another step down toward the driveway.

"Did you see it?" he asked, leaping from the truck.

Neither answered as they fell into each other's arms. They both already knew the answer, and it wasn't a good one.

Chapter 24

Booger couldn't sleep. Ever since he started spending more time at the Franks' house, studying up on their haunted leg bone or whatever it was, he'd had trouble sleeping.

He'd zonked out during his favorite show, woken up in his TV chair and stumbled into bed, only to toss and turn for hours on end. He kept thinking about that stupid bone. Why was it haunted? Whose was it? He studied every website and every blog about Native Americans and ghosts and haunting, and he had no answers.

And still he couldn't sleep.

He rolled over in his twisted sheets and glanced at the digital clock by his bed. It read 3:44 a.m. He yawned and sat up, feeling wide awake. He scratched his hair and slid out of his pajamas, trading them for cargo shorts and a *Haunted Happenings* T-shirt. He grabbed a cap to cover his "bed hair" and slipped on socks and shoes, then grabbed a flashlight from his desk drawer.

Next to his bed, Budweiser roused, but only enough to sniff before sliding his snout back onto his paws. It was just as well—he would only bark with excitement if he realized Booger was heading outside to the creek.

Booger crept silently past his mom's room. Her frequent shifts as a nurse at Heartland Hospital left her bone weary and, unfortunately for her, starved for sleep. Fortunately for Booger, when she did sleep, it was like the dead.

Knowing he would never get back to sleep, he grabbed a soda and a stale brownie from the fridge and devoured them both while slipping out the front door. He dropped the empty soda can in the recycling bin and, now that he was sure not to rouse the rest of his "family," Booger burped, long and low in the dark.

Booger hitched up his shorts and stood in his backyard, wondering what he was doing. He didn't know why, he just felt like the closer he got to the Franks' house, the better he'd feel.

Luckily, they didn't live too far. He followed Wolf Creek, his flashlight shining on the shallow ripples as he walked along the water's edge. The night was cool but damp, like it usually was this time of year.

Crickets chirped, mosquitoes buzzed and lights flickered in the Franks' house as Booger approached. He paused at the small line of trees that bordered the back of their property and watched as, inside, Wizzie polished the furniture in a frenzy.

Every light in the house was on, as usual, and he could hear classic rock thumping just inside the half-dozen or more sliding glass doors that circled the porch.

He felt bad, peeking in at her like that, even if she was his friend. He slipped back behind the line of thin, bare trees, wondering what to do next, when he heard it, soft and low, but there just the same.

It was the rhythmic chant of a Native war dance. "Eye, eye, eye, yah, eye, eye, eye, yah…" There was a tinkling sound that followed the rhythm, almost like a rattle. It was coming from the street where Wizzie and Booger saw the giant red wolf the first time.

Booger, his mouth dry, followed the sound using the lights from Wizzie's house to creep slowly, as the noise of the chanting increased and the rattling grew louder.

As Booger neared the front of the house, he slid along the exterior wall, clinging to it for safety. As he stood just off Wizzie's front porch, he saw the source of the sound: a young native brave, dressed only in moccasins and leather pants, whirling around, a stick in his hand, covered in dried animal bones tied together with leather thongs.

The young brave was handsome, with clean features and a strong body. He looked like a lot of the guys on the high school football team did after practice, sweaty and strong and confident. His eyes were closed as his lips moved, chanting softly in the cul-de-sac in front of Wizzie's house: "Eye, eye, eye, yah, eye, eye, eye, yah…"

The bones rattled and jingled, though Booger knew, just by the way the brave and his headdress flickered, it couldn't be real. And, knowing it wasn't real, Booger risked moving away from the house.

The air was colder now, and when Booger stepped on a dead, dry leaf, the brave stopped dancing and watched him standing there with his foot only half on the ground.

The brave watched him until Booger put his foot down and they both flinched at the sound of the crunching leaf. The brave took a step closer.

He waved his stick, the bones rattling in the cold, dark air. "Go. This house make leave," he said in broken English, voice young but haunting.

Whenever he spoke, the ghost brave flickered and shimmered as if it took so much of his ghostly energy he couldn't quite stay in human form and talk at the same time.

Booger shook his head, hardly believing his eyes or ears. "It's not my house," he said.

"Make them leave," Ghost Brave said, rattling his stick. "Make leave before Chief Running Blood make leave."

Booger gasped. "You mean…Chief Running Blood of the Mecklesh Clan?"

The ghost brave flared his nostrils. "What know of Mecklesh Clan?"

Booger was about to answer when the howling of a wolf interrupted him. Ghost Brave turned and inched away, turning back only once. "I leave Tala. She protect you," he said, nodding toward the trees where the giant red wolf glowed.

"Where are you going?" Booger asked. He wanted to follow the ghost brave but knew if he did, he would only turn to a cold, fine mist.

"Where you cannot follow," he said, and then disappeared into the trees. Before Booger could follow, the red wolf crept toward him.

Chapter 25

"I feel stupid," Billy said several nights later when he finally had a full night off work. Instead of sleeping, here he was on the front porch, holding hands with Wizzie and listening to Booger.

"You shouldn't be feeling anything," Booger said a little bluntly, nose buried in a thick book called *Conjuring for Beginners*. An awkward silence followed and when Booger looked up, he saw Billy's stern expression. "No, I mean…seriously, the book says you should be free of all feelings in order for your thoughts to be more powerful."

Billy smirked and ruffled the boy's hair, but Booger only frowned. "Both hands on the table, Mr. Frank," he instructed politely but firm. "If you would please take a seat."

"Okay, okay," said Billy, winking at Wizzie, but she was as stern and serious as young Booger.

"It won't work if you don't take it seriously," Wizzie scolded, none too playfully. "We all have to be of one mind for this to work, right, Booger?"

He smiled, pointing to a dog-eared page in his book. "That's what it says. Now, are we all ready?"

Wizzie nodded eagerly, clinging like a barnacle to Billy's left hand while Booger clutched Billy's right hand and waited for an answer.

"Yes, yes, for Pete's sake, let's get this done before some durn neighbor drives by and takes us all for fools."

Wizzie frowned. "It's midnight, Billy. Who's going to be driving in front of our house at this hour?"

"You guys…" Booger was anxious, and tugged gently on their hands like a little kid at the zoo eager to be done with lunch and head over to the monkey cage. "We're wasting time."

Wizzie tightened her grip on Billy's hand in a "mind your manners" way and, ever dutiful, Billy did as he was told. "Okay, okay," he said. "I'm serious this time. Work your magic, kid."

Booger nodded and looked to Wizzie, who agreed. "I'm ready, Booger."

He smiled and looked down at his book. "Close your eyes," he instructed, and Billy did. "Clear your mind." Billy tried. "Forget the modern times, and imagine this land as it once was."

Billy clenched his eyes shut. Booger's voice was growing more serious, almost manly.

"Imagine a land unspoiled by man, teeming with animal life, no cars, no buildings, no steam rising into the air, only the smoke of campfires, the creak of tents and the dance of this country's Native people."

Booger's voice grew somber, almost hypnotic. Despite his initial reluctance, Billy found himself picturing just such a scene: wide grasslands, clear creeks, Native American babies laughing, their mothers nursing, and warriors dancing, fresh from the hunt.

"This land is connected to its people," Booger said, voice almost unrecognizable. "This land is not our land, and it never was. A brave people, a mighty people, once ruled this land, and none was more powerful than Chief Running Blood."

Billy flinched at the name, for almost as quickly as Booger said it, the air around them grew chill and frosty. Billy was tempted to open his eyes, but Booger's voice convinced him to keep them closed.

"As more and more white men came to the south, looking for land and opportunity, taking not asking, Chief Running Blood earned his mighty title because he killed and butchered all those he saw, including his own braves if they disputed his bloody reign."

Billy shivered as a stiff breeze picked up, dusting leaves around the porch at their feet. Wizzie's hand grew cold in his but Booger was consumed now, hardly breathing as he roared, "To protect his land, Chief Running Blood would stop at nothing. Even swing his battle axe and slaughter his own people, pure blood or not. And now we are on his land and death will be to you."

Booger paused, wheezing, and Billy heard a faint rustling in the growing wind. He risked opening his eyes to find Booger pale and wan, sweat dotting his forehead, the pages of his book fluttering uselessly. His eyes were closed and his head was back.

He was not reading from the book. Someone, or something, was speaking through him.

Chapter 26

"Booger!" Wizzie shouted as the boy fell from his deck chair and slumped to the ground, mumbling, sweaty, and pale as a bed sheet. "Billy, help him up."

Billy hoisted Booger back into his chair where he slumped over on the table. Her heart pounded in the chilly air, the wind brisk as they looked at each other.

"What happened?" Billy asked over the wind. "What went wrong?"

"We should have never let him talk us into this." Wizzie fretted, pacing the length of the porch. "He's just a boy. What would his mama think?"

Booger moaned, rubbing his forehead. "What happened?" he asked, face green as if he'd gotten sick.

"What happened is you scared us both to death!" Wizzie berated him in a motherly tone.

He looked up and around, black hair whipping in the wind. She realized it was the first time she'd ever seen him without his faded *Haunted Happenings* ball cap on. "How?" he asked, standing up cautiously. "And when did it get so cold?"

"While you were speechifying to us about how we stole our land from the Native Americans," Billy said as brave as he could, as if to convince the rest of them he wasn't scared.

"I did what? What Native Americans? What land?"

Booger shivered, clutching himself. Wizzie kept waiting for the wind to die down but it had picked back up.

"You went on a tear," Billy said, pacing the porch with a concerned look on his face. "You don't remember that, Booger?"

"What?" Booger asked, and Wizzie grew concerned.

Booger looked back at her, eyes wide, confused and scared. His thick book of conjuring spells was lying open at his feet, the candles he'd lit and scattered around the table had all gone out and now they stood in anxious silence, shivering, with the wind whipping around them and moaning through the eaves.

Billy paused mid-pace and looked at Wizzie wide-eyed. "What— did you hear that?"

"Hear what?" Wizzie asked, loud enough to cover the beating of her heart because but she'd heard it: the moaning. It wasn't the wind, it was…something.

Or someone.

Booger stood, shivering in the chilly night air. "Look," he said, pointing a trembling finger into the darkness beyond their porch. Wizzie stood next to him, peering into the darkness, squinting to see what Booger did. Billy walked up beside her and grabbed her hand, for he had seen it, too.

"What?" she asked and, with his free hand, Billy pointed past the darkened cul-de-sac. There, shimmering amid the trembling saplings, stood a figure.

She gasped as it seemed to waver in and out of human form, but it was definitely a man. Ghostly, pale but not always, clearly Native

American, and towering nearly seven feet tall in his traditional headdress. He was bare-chested, with broad shoulders and muscular arms despite his advanced years.

He was laughing, not moaning. She heard it, a sound as deep as a moan, but thicker, faster, more rhythmic. His mouth was open, dark as the night that surrounded them. Billy had drawn her close into his arms, and Booger hovered near.

The shape drew near, whispering through the tree limbs, drifting like mist, bare feet never touching the ground.

"Inside," Billy ordered, yanking Wizzie to the left and through the open front door. "Booger, get in here!" He yanked Booger in, too, and they shut and locked the door.

The laughing increased, dark and violent, loud and cruel. It rattled the surrounding walls, it jiggled the doors, it roared until the lights flickered and the kitchen chairs rattled across the hardwood floor.

"Billy!" Wizzie gasped as the doorknob turned and the porch light flickered.

"Here," Billy said, dragging them both from the foyer and into the living room. The minute they were gone, the door bowed slightly inward with an awful pounding.

Pound. Pound. Boom. The door rattled, louder and louder, until the whole house began to shake around them. Knickknacks on the foyer table fell to the floor, cracking or breaking.

Wizzie didn't realize she was crying until Billy gripped her tight. "It's okay," he lied. "We're fine."

The pounding continued, the floors trembled, the walls shook, and pictures hung on the walls turned crooked from the force. She put her hands over her ears but it did little good. She could still feel the pounding under her feet, up through her legs, deep in her bones.

And suddenly it all stopped. The silence that followed was almost worse as they stood, shivering in the middle of the living room, waiting for what might happen next.

Wizzie's heart was pounding. Billy was holding her tight and, as she turned to stare up at him, Booger dashed from their side and raced for the door. "Booger!" she cried out, but it was too late.

He threw open the door and stood in the doorway, fists clenched at his sides. "We're not afraid of you!" he shouted into the darkness.

Billy and Wizzie raced to his side. Wizzie looked out and saw the porch, the cul-de-sac, the street itself was empty, quiet and still.

"You don't scare us!" Booger shouted, face red, tears running down his cheeks. His voice was cracking as he bellowed, "We're not alone, you hear? You didn't come back alone! They will stop you, we will stop you. We're not alone!"

"Get in here, Booger." Billy yanked the boy back inside. Without prompting, he hugged him tight, patting his back as the young boy burst into tears. "It's okay, Booger," he soothed, looking to Wizzie helplessly. "It's over, we're here, we're safe."

But even as Billy said the words, Wizzie knew they weren't true. Whatever had pounded on their door and shook their house to the core wasn't going away so easily.

No matter what Billy said to make Booger feel better.

Chapter 27

"Are you sure, honey?" Wizzie's sister, Eve, asked as they talked late into the Sunday evening. "I mean, I don't want to intrude on the honeymooners or anything."

"Oh, please," Wizzie said, blushing, waving her hand even though Eve was all the way in South Carolina. "You know Billy loves you, girl."

"He may love me, but does he want me as a houseguest so soon after moving in? What about Lily? Will she be coming, too, Wizzie?"

"No, sugar, she is still in Europe with boyfriend number—what is it? Number nine or ten?"

Eve laughed. "Who's counting anymore?"

"Besides, she still has not forgiven me for getting custody of the two of you after Mom and Dad died."

"That's not true, Wizzie. She has always felt the three of us would have been better off if she and I went to live with Mom's uncle."

"Eve, it didn't feel right, he was too, too…strange, and besides, Mom told me the weekend before she…um, passed to stay away from him."

"She did?"

"Yes, she did. And, Eve, you were only twelve and Lily just fifteen. I couldn't do it. I couldn't send you to live with them, I didn't know them."

"But, Wizzie, Great Aunt Bessie was so sweet."

"I know she was, but that was also a deciding reason. It appeared to me that he didn't treat her so well either."

Weeks had passed without an incident; no cold air, no chills, no moaning or Native American words scrawled on walls or glowing red wolves. Now that life had somewhat returned to normal, Wizzie was desperate to see her younger sister, Eve.

Tall and athletic, with honey-blond curls down to her waist and deep blue eyes, Eve had been thick as thieves with Wizzie growing up. Then Eve went off to college to study journalism and Wizzie met Billy and, well, one thing led to another.

It had been almost six months since they'd seen each other, a record for the two sisters.

Wizzie chuckled. "We've lived here for three months, Eve!"

Her sister laughed, warm and sweet, just like her. "Then my housewarming present is long overdue. I can blow off classes tomorrow and spend a long weekend, will that do?"

As she hung up the phone, Wizzie hadn't felt this excited since she and Billy had moved into the house on Wolf Creek. She set off straight away to the grocery store for some of Eve's favorite foods. As she strolled through the aisles, grabbing crunchy peanut butter and cinnamon raisin bread, Ruffles chips and onion dip, she finally felt at ease in her skin.

The sun was out, the day was new and she felt the burden of stress and anxiety lift off her shoulders as she splurged and bought a few steaks to grill out on their porch.

On the way home she stopped at a roadside stand and got fresh strawberries for breakfast, and fresh flowers for the nightstand in Eve's guest room. As she was looking at a basket of peaches, she noticed in her peripheral vision that it was there again, the black-on-black truck, but what was it doing here? Grabbing her purchases, she turned and walked straight into another shopper. Dark sunglasses looked down at her, and he smiled.

"Oh, gosh, I'm so sorry. I wasn't paying attention to where I was going." Wizzie rolled her eyes at herself and blushed.

He smiled again, bent and picked up the flowers he'd knocked out of her hand. "No worries. No damage done."

She straightened her skirt, turned and looked behind her. The black truck was gone. She blinked and looked around. Where did the guy go? Wizzie shook her head.

At home she put fresh linens on the guest bed and aired out the house, letting in the cool autumn breeze as she set about sprucing up the place with dabs of color here and there.

Billy came home as Wizzie was marinating the steaks and grabbed a hug from her and a cube of cheese from the appetizer platter.

"Oh, you." She giggled in high spirits as he grabbed himself a beer and topped off her glass of wine. "I wish you worked dayshift all the time." Wizzie frowned.

"So do I. I'm just happy the boss let me change shifts for Eve's visit." Billy smiled.

Wizzie gave him a quick kiss on the lips. "Go clean up before she gets here."

He groaned half-jokingly and whined, "Do I have to?" Her strict look was all the answer he needed, and he bounded up the stairs.

She was just setting out the cheese and fruit platter when the doorbell rang. She saw Eve's curly blond hair through the glass inset and squealed, running into the foyer and springing open the door for a long-awaited sisterly bear hug.

"You look so cute," Wizzie said as she ushered Eve in, lugging several bags behind her.

"Me?" she said, whirling about the living room. "Check out this place, Wizzie! It's huge!"

Wizzie chuckled and gave Eve a quick tour of the downstairs before the two girls shuffled off to the porch to catch up on girl talk, family gossip and everything and anything in between.

Candles flickered on the patio, wine flowed and Billy sauntered out, freshly scrubbed and dressed to impress in pressed jeans and the new red sweater Wizzie picked out especially for her sister's visit.

Wizzie had just finished telling Eve about the hauntings.

"So, Billy, what can I expect in the middle of the night?" Eve asked. "A huge red wolf slobbering at my feet or a Native American chanting at the foot of my bed?"

"Just keep it up," Billy snickered, waving his half-empty beer in her general direction, "and I'll have our neighbor summon up a ghost that'll scare your pants off!"

"Oh, Billy." Wizzie snorted, but she laughed as well. She felt the worst was behind them, family was here and she could finally call her new house "home."

Chapter 28

Booger was playing with Budweiser down by the creek when he heard a splash and a giggle. He crept along the riverbank, Budweiser panting by his side, until he heard more splashing and emerged from the tree line to see a blond woman retrieving a fishing pole from the shallow creek bed.

"Need some help?" Booger asked as Budweiser bounded forward, licking the woman's legs and making her giggle even more.

"No thanks," she said in a southern drawl that sounded a lot like Booger's neighbors, the Frank family. "Your horse is about all I can handle at the moment."

"Budweiser!" Booger cried, but the woman seemed to like the attention and, after all, Budweiser easily swam out into the water and grabbed the fishing pole, bringing it back on dry land.

"I could never have done that," the woman said, sliding onto her backside on the dew-covered riverbank. "I'm Eve, by the way. Wizzie is my sister."

"Oh," Booger said, sitting down next to her as she petted Budweiser on the head. "I thought you sounded familiar."

She chuckled and held out a dog-drool-covered-hand. "You must be...Booger?"

Booger chuckled and shook slimy hands with her. "You mean the Franks warned you about me?"

"Not so much warned," Eve said, still chuckling as Budweiser finally nestled down between them. "More like...prepared."

"I'm pretty harmless," he said, wondering why he seemed to spend more time talking to grown-ups than kids his own age.

Eve smiled and patted his hand. "Actually, honey, they said you've been a big help to them these last few weeks. In fact, I probably wouldn't be here visiting if you hadn't cleansed the house of all its spirits."

He blushed, looking out at her from under the protective brim of his *Haunted Happenings* cap. "You seem pretty brave to me. I bet you would have come anyway."

"Not me," she said, waving her hands in front of her. "I'm a big fat wimp when it comes to all that monkey business."

"Do you believe in ghosts?" he asked.

Budweiser slid his snout on his paws, sighing as if he'd heard this all before.

"I never really thought about it much until Wizzie started going through her troubles," she said. "I guess, until I see it with my own eyes, I'm still not sure that I do."

"Pray you don't," Booger said, shivering at the thought. "I've watched about a million haunted house shows in my life so far, and I've never seen anything like what they've been going through."

Eve nodded, smiling. "But it's not just them going through it, is it, honey? I hear you've had your ups and downs as well."

Booger didn't deny it. "It's been scary at times, for sure, and I've seen stuff with or without the Franks around." He nodded toward their backyard, big and sprawling as the sun came up. "But it's all coming from there. For whatever reason, and we're still trying to figure it out, most of the activity seems to be centered around that house."

Eve clasped her shoulders as if shivering. "But you did that séance, right, Booger? And since then nothing, right?"

Booger nodded, shivering himself as he thought back to that long, dark night. "No, you're right. And I hope that took care of everything…"

His voice trailed off, but Eve was as sharp and savvy as her sister, Wizzie. "You hope?" she asked, one eyebrow arched curiously. "You're not sure?"

Booger smiled wryly, feeling weary in his young bones. "These are ghosts we're dealing with, Eve. You're never sure."

She smirked, but her eyes were serious. "You're scaring me, sugar," she drawled. "From the way Wizzie and Billy talked, it sounded like their house was from some kind of fairy tale dream, or horror story."

Booger nodded energetically. "I'm not trying to scare anybody, Eve, really I'm not. But if you'd seen what I've seen, if you'd stood in that hallway hearing a ghostly Indian chief shaking the whole house with his pounding, you'd know that things like that just don't… go away…because you want them to."

They both nodded, lost in their own thoughts. Booger still wasn't sleeping, and he kind of kept waiting for the other shoe to drop. As much as Wizzie and Billy floated around the house, fluffing up throw pillows and lighting candles and cooking out, he felt they were just pushing away the dark thoughts and living it up while they could.

"Do you think me being here…" She paused as she looked off into the distance. "Might…upset this Indian chief?"

Booger saw the tightness in her face, the clenching of her jaw, and felt bad for spooking her. He brightened, sat up a little straighter and changed tack.

"Naw," he said, waving a hand dismissively. "If anything, you'll probably hold him off for as long as you stay. From my readings, it's clear that ghosts resist change. They're used to haunting us here, same time every night, same way. You being new to the mix, you're probably doing Wizzie and Billy a big favor."

She seemed to float with relief, standing up and dusting off the backs of her cutoff jeans. "Phew," she said, helping him up as Budweiser sprang to attention and licked her hand. "You had me going there for a minute, ghost hunter!"

He smiled, waving her off. "No need to worry," he said as she took her fishing pole, still dripping, and headed for the back steps of the porch.

Now if only he could convince himself.

Chapter 29

She is running, rain pounding on her head, blond hair in disarray as she stumbles through the mud. It's like the end of the world, the sky dark, clouds blotting out the moon, rain so thick she can barely see.

And everywhere, on all sides, the sound of rushing water. Her lungs are burning as she strains for more air; she can't get enough. His footsteps are right behind her, thick and inhuman; they simply can't be real.

And yet whenever she looks back through the rain she can just make out the figure of an Indian chief. He is impossibly tall, rain splashing off his elaborate headdress, a wooden necklace clattering on his bare chest, a giant war axe in his hand.

He chants something unintelligible, drowned out by the thunder and the rain and the lightning and the water. And then, in front of her, is a small wooden bridge, railings wet with rushing water as it threatens to overtake the tiny foothold.

She races for it but pauses, bare feet on wet wood, turning for just a second to look back. The Indian chief is gone, but the rain is blinding, and every inch of her is soaked. She crumbles to the ground, clinging to the trembling bridge for support as she breathes in and out great gasping gulps of wet, rainy air.

And then the crackling of his wooden necklaces, the swinging of his war axe and the chanting return, closer than ever. She cries, rising, and races onto the bridge, flimsy and slippery beneath her bare feet. She bites her lower lip to keep from screaming as the chanting comes closer, closer, closer...

Eve woke with a start, heart pounding, body trembling, covered in sweat. She clutched the sheets twisted around her legs, and stared around the room, disoriented.

Moonlight trickled through half-open blinds, illuminating a distressed white bureau across from the bed and two matching nightstands on either side of it.

The sheets were powder blue, and the pillows she'd mangled were navy, drenched in her sweat, with one lying at her feet. She rubbed her head and wondered where she was until it hit her: *Wizzie!*

She groaned and buried her face in her hands. Her skin was burning, sweat slick on her forehead, and her chest still pounding from the nightmare. She turned, untangled her thighs from the damp, twisted sheets and put her bare feet on the cold, hardwood floor.

"Take it down a notch, Eve," she whispered to herself, breathing more steadily now, smirking gently in the night. "It was just a nightmare. You're in Wizzie's new house, you're fine...you're safe..."

She stood on wobbly legs, padded softly across the floor, and opened the blinds to see the moon full, not a cloud in the sky, no sign of rain for miles and miles. She sagged against the wall, staring down into the yard, which was soft and green and the opposite of muddy.

She sighed with relief, openly and loudly, before a tight, anxious chuckle escaped her clenched throat. There was a small terry cloth robe hanging from a knob on the closet door and she grabbed it, turning to face the little digital clock by her bed as she slipped into her fluffy pink slippers.

She groaned. The clock read 4:22 a.m. and, as wired as she was, Eve knew there was no chance of her getting back to sleep this night. She crept through the door, treading lightly in the upstairs hall, uncertain of where the floorboards might creak and groan beneath her feet.

She slipped past her sister's room. The door was closed, Billy was snoring inside and there was not another sound in the house. She sighed, desperate for a little company, for Wizzie's soft voice, her warm hands, and her comforting words.

As little girls, Wizzie always soothed Eve's mind after a bad dream. What she wouldn't do for a little sisterly advice and hot cocoa right about now. Instead she crept down the stairs in the dark, worrying over every creak and crack, until she found herself in the kitchen.

She heated up a cup of microwave coffee and, unable to find the sweetener, drank it black with a swirl of milk to soften the bitter taste.

The house was quiet and still, the living room vast and open, airy and uncluttered. She sighed, carefully opened the sliding glass door and inched onto the porch.

With the heavy glass door shut behind her, Eve finally relaxed, knowing she could walk and traipse and slip and slurp without the noise disturbing Wizzie and her sleeping husband.

She sighed again, slipping down into a soft deck chair and cradling her coffee cup in both hands. The night was cool, but she had her robe and pulled it tighter against her, letting the coffee do its thing as the soft tides of Wolf Creek lapped gently against the shoreline.

She could smile now, heart rate finally returning to normal, but the power of the nightmare still lingered. It had all felt so real, from the rain against her cheek to the mud between her toes, she could hardly believe it wasn't raining.

Chapter 30

Thunder wakes him, a crack so close it sounds like it's right next to his ear. He bolts up in bed just as a streak of lightning turns the middle of the night into broad daylight.

He turns, rubbing his eyes, rain pelting his bedroom window as he stumbles over a catcher's mitt and his schoolbooks. He puts his nose to the glass as thunder grumbles again. In the flash of lightning to follow he sees her: a woman, blond hair plastered against her head, nightgown soaked, feet bare, trampling through the mud.

He calls out to her, screaming, banging on the window to alert her to the shape at her back: tall, muscular, fast, the Indian, Chief Running Blood, waving a bloody hatchet at her back.

He opens the window, rain flooding his room, and climbs out, bare feet in mud so thick he finds it hard to follow. He cries out in the rain, but the wind is so strong it takes his words and scatters them far and wide.

He runs as fast as he can—which isn't very with his feet stuck every few inches—waving his arms. Chief Running

Blood speeds away, moccasins barely touching the ground. The girl screams, stumbling to her knees, grabs a tree by the creek bed and draws herself up.

Another sound swells to his right: Wolf Creek cresting its banks. His bare feet splash through the muck as the water rages, gurgling, roiling, and they approach the tiny wooden bridge that leads to the next subdivision and onward into town.

He stumbles to his knees, hands palms down in the mud. The rain is so thick he can taste it. He is drenched to the skin, watching as she reaches the bridge.

He turns, the sound of a rushing wave—a wave!—to his right as the creek surges like raging river rapids and not the place he's fished four hundred times without so much as a ripple.

"No!" he cries out, waving with muddy hands, feet so deep in the mud he literally can't stand. "No, no, the bridge, the bridge..."

But it's no use. The water rushes, she stumbles onto the bridge and the water takes her and the bridge in a froth of white waves that crash and boil and bubble until there's nothing left to mark where they once stood.

He pounds the mud, calling out, blinking back the tears, blinking out the stinging rain, when he hears muddy footsteps and stares at the water's edge where Chief Running Blood turns to him wearing a smile.

With effortless ease the bloody chief raises his right hand and lets loose the battle axe. The blade slices right through the raindrops as it flies and flies and...

Booger woke with a start, hands over his face, panting and screaming and crying all at once. He bolted upright in his bed, sheets twisted and damp around his legs.

The door burst open and his mother stumbled in, one arm stuffed in her robe, the other dangling at her side. "Booger!" she shouted from the doorway. "What is it? What's wrong?"

He shook his head, voice coming out shaky and raw. "I'm sorry, Mom," he said, still panting from the power of his dream. "A nightmare, I guess?"

She frowned, sagging against the doorjamb. "Another one, honey? We're going to have to go see someone if this keeps going on. That's your third this week."

"I know, Mom," he said, nodding. "I just…too many scary movies, I guess."

She frowned, suspicious, but it was late—past 4 a.m. or so it said on the clock by his bed—and she had to work in the morning. "You good now?" she asked.

He smiled, lying through his teeth. "I'm fine, Mom, really. Go back to sleep."

She wavered in the doorway, looking relieved, and finally shrugged, yawning. "I love you, Booger." She slouched away. "And you, too, Budweiser," she called over her shoulder, the dog barely rousing as he lay nestled under Booger's desk.

"Some best friend," he grumbled, slipping from his bed. The chocolate lab finally lifted his head—barely—licked his lips, whined a little and went right back to sleep.

Booger looked at the clock again, frowning. There was no way he'd get back to sleep tonight. At least it was Saturday morning, though still hours before sunrise.

He sat on the edge of his bed, wiped the sweat from his brow and tried to scrub the images of his nightmare from his brain, but there was no way. It felt so real he could practically hear the waters of Wolf Creek rising outside his window.

He dressed quickly and slipped through his window, shutting it carefully so Budweiser wouldn't follow. The ground was dry and soft beneath his feet, not wet at all.

He paused by the shores of the creek, listening, and heard barely a ripple. He was about to turn around and sneak back inside his room when he heard a sliding glass door open in the predawn stillness.

There was only one house close enough to hear something like that, and he paused, wondering if he should tell Wizzie about his dream. She was fairly certain Chief Running Blood was gone, but after this dream, Booger wondered.

His mom wasn't lying; for the last three nights he'd been woken up, shouting, because of stupid Chief Running Blood. Maybe… maybe something happened during that séance, something Booger couldn't control.

Maybe Chief Running Blood left something behind that night, before he left them all clinging and shaking in the middle of the living room. Maybe he left something behind…in Booger.

Maybe that was why he was having these dreams. Maybe that was why he couldn't sleep. He crept closer to the Franks' porch. A soft light burned, candle flames flickering as someone raised a large white coffee mug to her face.

As he crept near, careful not to spook her, Booger saw it wasn't Wizzie sitting there after all, but her sister, Eve. Petite and blond, she sat in a bathrobe, knees pulled high to her chest, eyes wide as she peered out past the porch railing into the placid waters of Wolf Creek.

Booger knew better than to step out from the tree line and scare her, and he was about to turn around and backtrack his way home when the sliding glass door opened once more.

This time it was Wizzie, rattled and shaking, frantic, with one arm in her robe just like Booger's mom had stood in his doorway a few minutes before.

"Wizzie!" Eve gasped, turning around and standing, concern in her high-pitched voice. "Whatever's gotten into you?"

"W-w-why are you sitting out here?" Wizzie asked. Slowly, Booger crept from the tree line. She spotted him right away, eyes wide and on high alert. "Booger? What…whatever are you doing out here this time of night?"

"I could ask you both the same thing," he said, thinking he sounded very adult.

Eve turned once more, looking at him, then back to Wizzie. "I…I had a dream," she said, putting down her coffee mug and pacing slightly, halfway toward Booger then back to Wizzie, but not too close, then back toward Booger, and then back again. "It woke me up."

"Me, too!" Booger and Wizzie said at the same time.

Wizzie crept forward and sank into a deck chair as if she might not be able to stand otherwise. Eve followed her, picking up her oversized mug and clinging to it protectively.

"What was yours about?" Eve asked, wide-eyed, her voice soft.

Wizzie looked at Booger and replied, "Water, lots and lots of water."

But as Booger and Eve both nodded, he knew Wizzie wasn't telling the whole story. And he couldn't quite blame her. With Eve's teeth chattering, her knuckles white around the coffee mug, maybe tonight wasn't the night to talk about Chief Running Blood.

Chapter 31

Billy woke, gasping, and clutched at the collar of his V-neck T-shirt. It was drenched in sweat and he looked down instinctively to find Wizzie fast asleep.

He was relieved, despite the pounding of his heart. She'd been on edge so often lately, he hated even turning over in his sleep for fear of waking her. Now he slid from the twisted sheets as carefully as possible, noting the digital clock on the nightstand that read 4:18 a.m.

He slipped from the room, mindful to grab his robe now that Wizzie's sister was staying with them. He paused outside the guest room door, standing silently until he heard the rhythm of her heavy breathing. Then he padded downstairs and poured himself a giant glass of orange juice.

There were donuts, too. Wizzie had gone out and gotten all kinds of treats for Eve but the two were always so worried about their weight the donuts sat untouched.

Until now. Billy sat in the breakfast nook, not bothering to turn on the lights for fear one of the girls would see it and get alarmed. They'd been having bad dreams lately, dreams of water and floods, and no matter what Billy tried to tell them about the impossibility of those kinds of things happening this late in the fall, the girls' nerves just wouldn't be calmed.

He sat quietly in the dark, enjoying the peace. Billy loved Wizzie's sister, but when the two got together, boy howdy could those gals talk! And talk and talk and talk and talk…

He grabbed a chocolate donut. There was no hope of him getting back to sleep tonight anyway. He was there, minding his own business, when the glow outside the kitchen window appeared.

He discounted it at first. There was always a low mist in the early morning around Wolf Creek. He and Wizzie had got used to it with his new hours at the plant and her cleaning the house all night, and so at first Billy hoped—oh, how he hoped—it was just one of the busy mosquito trucks buzzing through the cul-de-sac or the taillights of a car delivering papers at this ungodly hour.

But the glow grew fiery and persistent, filling Billy's gut with dread. He dropped the rest of his uneaten donut back to his plate, stood, and inched closer toward the window.

The house was dark, leaving no reflection in the glass as Billy peered out. What he saw made him flinch. Chief Running Blood was there, chanting in the darkness; a glowing giant swirling in the mist, with one knee up, his head down, a bloody hatchet in one hand and a noisy stick in the other.

His headdress was magnificent, flowing and feathery, as he whirled and danced amid the trees that bordered their property. Billy found his fists balled at his sides as he drifted to the door, not giving himself time to pause as he flung it open and slid it shut quietly at his back.

He walked down the steps and into the drive forcefully, calling out in a hissed whisper, "Hey!" His bare feet crunched in the gravel just beyond his drive and he called again. "Hey! You!"

The glowing vision didn't stop, or slow, or respond in any way. Billy continued to move closer more slowly, and the sudden chill in the air made him wrap his arms around his torso as he drew near enough to see the bones rattling on the chief's ornately carved stick and the dried blood on his war hatchet.

"Leave my family alone!" Billy shouted when he stopped five or six feet away. He felt so frustrated, fists at his sides, bare feet in the gravel, shivering in the ghost's cold mist.

If it was a man, he could go to war, pounding him with his fists or punching him in the face. Even if the guy got the best of him, at least Billy could send a message not to mess with him anymore. Or he could call the cops, or a few of his buddies from the plastics plant, and teach the guy a good, old-fashioned lesson in not messing with another man's family.

But this…this…ghost thing, this specter, this vision, Billy couldn't do a durn thing about it. He couldn't punch it, couldn't kick it, couldn't wish it or wash it or threaten it away. So he stood, shouting at it in the middle of the night, knowing it would do little.

And then, mid-rant, the bloody chief looked up, eyes redder than the rest of him, glowing like hot coals in the center of his face. The glare was so intense Billy took an involuntary step back, and then another as the chief seemed to float on the very mist and follow him toward his front doorstep.

"Leave here now, white man," the chief bellowed, each of his words punctuated by a burst of cold air splashing across Billy's face. "Before too late!"

Billy huddled near the bottom step, clinging to the railing as the mist swirled and the chief disappeared. Billy stood a little taller, risking a step toward where the giant ghost had just thundered little clouds of red mist into his face.

Without warning, the sky opened and rain began falling in a heavy, freezing downpour. Billy stood, stunned and shivering, noting that the rest of the lawn, even the cul-de-sac, was still dry.

Chapter 32

Wizzie heard what sounded like thunder and woke, startled to see the bed empty. The clock read nearly 5 a.m. and she rose, slipped into her robe and drifted out into the hall.

She felt wide awake and listened closely for the sound that had roused her out of a deep slumber, the best sleep Wizzie had had all week. She crept down each stair, not wanting to disturb her sister, Eve. Once in the kitchen, she spotted a half-eaten donut and empty glass of orange juice on the breakfast nook table. She frowned, thinking Billy might have slipped out onto the porch but then she heard the splatter of rain on the front stoop.

She frowned again and stared out the kitchen window at a clear, dark sky. As she moved toward the door she heard whimpering and raced to open it, finding Billy standing there, drenched from head to toe, shivering and crying silently under his own little rain cloud.

She raced down the steps and, almost as if the rain had been waiting for her, it stopped, slowing to a fine trickle before the sky dried out completely. Billy looked at her, eyes wild and wet, wiping them with a drenched sleeve as he slumped to the bottom step.

"Goodness gracious," she gasped, sitting down next to him, the steps wet and ruining the seat of her new robe. "What happened, Billy?"

He was breathless and trembling, gasping for air. With his hair drenched around his head he looked like a drowned rat. He turned to her, eyes wide. "It was him, Wizzie, that stupid Chief Running Blood!"

"Here?" she asked, unconsciously inching back from him. "But how? When? Why?" Now she sounded pitiful, in need of rescue, voice high and soft and whiny. "I thought...why is this all happening to us again, Billy?"

He turned to her then, eyes sadder, softer. "I wish I knew, honey."

"What should we do?" she asked, voice cracking with emotion. "Should we move?"

Billy's eyes hardened and his teeth set, making the muscles in his jaw flex. "That's what he told us to do," he said. "That's what he wants."

"I don't want to leave, Billy, but...what if something happens to you? Like tonight? What if he'd done more than soak you? I could never live with myself..."

He took her into his arms, getting her all wet but she couldn't have cared less. Just to feel him next to her, to be held in his strong arms, cold and trembling though they might have been, made Wizzie instantly feel better. "Think of how I feel, Wizzie, leaving you alone here at night all the time."

She shook her head. "I just don't see any way around it, Billy. We bought this home, we worked hard to afford it. I just don't see us letting some spirit take it away from us."

His eyes leapt hopefully, searching hers. "Really? Because that's how I felt tonight, shouting at that Chief Running Blood."

She stood up, reached for his hand, and dragged him along with her. "Then it's settled," she said, a great weight lifting from her shoulders. "You and I both agree, Billy, that our home is where we belong, and that no durn spirit from another time is going to take it from us, right?"

He smiled, looking adorably pitiful in his dripping robe and sopping hair. "I couldn't agree more, baby. Maybe, maybe we've been going about this all wrong. Maybe cowering in the shadows and running from this thing isn't working. Tonight, Wizzie, I yelled at that old chief. I shouted at him to leave us alone. That's when he turned and rained on me…"

They both chuckled as Billy ran his long, pale fingers through his dripping mop of hair. "Maybe we just need to combine our strength to beat this sucker, Wizzie!"

She got him inside, into the laundry room. "God, I hope so, Billy. I can't take much more of this."

"Me neither." His lips were blue and his chin trembled as he stared over her head at something in the distance. "I can't take much more," he mumbled as she helped him out of his wet clothes and into fresh boxers and a soft, warm T-shirt. "And I won't take any more!"

Chapter 33

Eve stood in the doorway, clinging to the bathrobe knotted around her tiny waist. "No, you two go on," she said, voice Southern and sweet. "You've both been waiting on me hand and foot all week; you deserve a nice night out."

Wizzie stood at the bottom of the steps, the pretty blue shawl Eve gave her wrapped around her shoulders. The night was chilly but clear. Wizzie frowned and said, "But we wanted to take you to our favorite restaurant in town, Eve. That's what tonight was all about."

"I know that," Eve said, wrinkling her nose. "But with my bad dreams and all this mess about Chief What's His Name, I'm just plum tuckered. Plus I've got that long drive tomorrow. Naw, you two go on, have a nice evening and..." She winked at Billy, who blushed. "I won't wait up for you two love birds."

Billy shook his head and said, "Darling, we've got all our life to have romantic dinners for two. Eve, we'd really like for you to join us."

He sounded sincere, and Eve was happy Wizzie had found a good man who would welcome his wife's family as much as he welcomed her. "Thanks for saying that, hon, but I'll take a rain check."

They argued a bit more, but finally Eve convinced them that there really wasn't a "going out to dinner" dress under her terry cloth robe and Billy and Wizzie drove away in his beloved pickup truck. She smiled to see them happy and content in their new life, then shut the door and brewed herself a cup of tea.

Fact was, as much as she loved the big new house and all the little touches Wizzie threw together to turn it into a home, Eve was looking forward to getting back to her own little apartment. Nice as the house was, she'd never felt a place so oppressive and gloomy in all her life.

She shivered even as she warmed her hands around the fresh cup of tea and traipsed through the cozy living room to linger on the porch. She took in the briny scent of Wolf Creek as she settled into her favorite deck chair and watched the darkness creep across the land.

The tea was strong, but that's just how she wanted it. Tired as she was, Eve had a lot of packing to do. Not only had Wizzie washed and folded all her clothes, but she bestowed upon Eve the usual gamut of homemade gifts for the trip home: throw pillows to match the ones Eve had admired on Wizzie's porch, a knitted scarf, bath towels, the list went on.

Eve was happy to know that her sister was in a good place even if her durn old house was haunted. As if on cue, the sound of thunder rumbled in the distance but Eve ignored it purposefully, refusing to believe that dreams came to life.

She sat and sipped at her tea, sternly staring into the line of scruffy pines that lined the shore, ignoring the flashes of lightning that danced in the distance. She pictured instead Wizzie and Billy on their date, holding hands in the firelight, ordering a bottle of wine they couldn't afford because whatever they did or didn't know, those two knew how to create memories—special ones.

The wind blew up, extinguishing the candles Eve always liked to light and making her burrow deeper into the fuzzy blue robe Wizzie had had waiting on her guest bed when Eve first arrived to stay. Warm as it was, it failed to keep out the chilling cold that seemed to have come from nowhere.

Eve stood, blinking into the darkness as the sound of rainfall, heavy and thick, splashed in Wolf Creek and splattered on the bottom porch steps. She made a little squeak sound as the swirling wind dashed the rain into the porch, spraying her face as she stumbled back to reach for the sliding glass door.

She'd left it open to catch the evening breeze and freshen up the house with the crisp night air, but as she went to step inside the open door it slid shut right before her eyes.

She squawked, hand at her throat, and turned to race for the next one. It, too, slammed shut, as did the other four in the wraparound porch—slam, slam, slam, slam! She stood helpless on the porch, tugging on the last door, trying in vain to slide it open as it remained steadfastly shut.

The storm had moved in, the rain a steady drumbeat on the porch's tin roof by now, and the wind was swirling around, tossing throw pillows and toppling pillar candles and spilling her tea. She tried door after door frantically and none would budge.

Inside the house the kitchen light shone on a peaceful setting, the living room furniture was arranged just so, throw pillows fluffed and angled perfectly, the coffee table freshly polished and women's magazines arranged neatly in a pile.

Outside, Eve was already half-drenched, blond hair scraggly, bathrobe splattered and stained with cold, stinging rain. The moon shone bright between angry gray clouds as she considered her dilemma. She was locked out of the porch, but perhaps she could try the front door. She was almost sure she hadn't locked it when Wizzie and Billy left.

She approached the edge of the porch cautiously, the rain so strong it stung her eyes to stare at the white caps on Wolf Creek and the thin pine trees bent over from the storm. Already her feet were dripping, the clean porch deck covered in an inch of rain water. The wicker end chair had overturned and was scraping toward the sliding glass doors as the wind whipped the other furniture here and there.

She could only imagine the glass doors shattering in the gale force winds, shards slashing her skin to ribbons if she waited on the porch any longer.

She gritted her teeth and slid down the porch steps, bare feet landing in cold mud, and trudged along the back wall of the house toward the front door. Garbage cans were overturned, and all Wizzie's carefully tended potted plants were whipped and broken from the front stoop railing.

She tugged on the door but now it was locked and wouldn't budge. She began crying, but couldn't feel the tears for the stinging rain lashing at her cheeks. It was just like the dream, only colder, angrier, stronger.

The rain was freezing and hard against her skin, and her robe did little to keep the constant battering waves of water from the flimsy nightgown she wore underneath.

She turned toward the cul-de-sac, eager to get as far away from the river as possible. Her bare feet crunched over wet gravel when she heard a low, grisly moan. At first she thought it was the storm and trudged forth bravely, but with each step the howl grew louder, more forceful, more…personal.

"Eve," it said, low and ghastly. When she glanced up he was standing there, towering over her, glowing red: the bloody Indian chief! He held a ghostly axe above his head, the dangerous blade covered with blood and gore.

She screamed, turning and running in the only direction left to her, toward the river. With each step her heart pounded, the mud creeping between her frozen toes as she ran. The ghost of Chief Running Blood remained right behind her as, just in the distance, a bridge called out to her, offering sweet relief from her ghostly, ghastly pursuer.

Chapter 34

Booger was doing his homework, finally, when Budweiser began chomping at the bit, scratching at the windowsill, desperate to get out. "What is it, boy?" Booger asked, approaching the glass and throwing it open so he could see whatever it was Budweiser was so desperate to chase.

A cold gust of wind blew in, damp with evening rain. Suddenly, in the distance, the rumble of thunder and a spit of lightning just over Wolf Creek made both Budweiser and his master blink.

"You're not going out there!" Booger said, reaching for the window, but Budweiser was nothing if not persistent—and agile. He leapt up and over the windowsill, landing in the dirt, and turned to face Booger.

Budweiser barked and nodded his big brown head toward the riverbed.

Booger was frightened. The thunder, the lightning, the darkness of night, the threatening rain, it was much too much like his dream to follow Budweiser along Wolf Creek.

But suddenly the dog darted just out of view, and Booger knew he had to give chase. He grabbed his jacket and cap, glad his mom was working another late shift at the hospital, and followed his trusty chocolate lab up and over the sill and onto the wet, frosty ground.

As if it had been waiting for him, the wind gusted and the rain pounced, drenching Booger in an instant it was so heavy, thick and driving. Budweiser was just ahead, tail and tongue wagging, waiting for Booger to reach his side. The minute he did, he tore up toward the Franks' residence.

"Great" Booger thought, shivering from more than just the rain as he struggled to follow. He would have pinched himself to see if this was all really happening, but the rain stinging his eyes and pelting his skin, the mud holding him back, the freezing night air and the rising river all told him this was real. It was happening to him right now!

Budweiser barked up in the distance. He was too fast for Booger to keep up with, particularly with mud up to his ankles and his shoes practically buried in the lawn. Partly the water was rain, but not all. He risked a glance to his right side and saw, with a double extra heart pound and wide open eyes, the creek rising over its bed.

"But how?" he mumbled to himself, voice caught on the wind and whisked away as he finally reached the Franks' porch. It was empty and in tatters, with furniture toppled and throw pillows floating on an inch or two of rippling rain water.

Just then the wind shifted and sent a red pillar candle flying down the steps, landing at Booger's feet. He flinched, as if it was perhaps a body part or bloody knife, and Budweiser barked urgently, stridently, before a yelp caught in his throat.

"Budweiser!" Booger yelled, racing to the sound of the noise only to find his drenched chocolate lab standing at the edge of the Franks' yard, nose pointed off in the distance toward Dead Man's Cliff.

"No," Booger choked, squinting to see the glowing form of Chief Running Blood giving chase. And there, just in front of him, clinging to the blue robe from his living nightmare, was Wizzie's sister, Eve.

"No!" he shouted more forcefully now, giving chase. He turned, expecting his faithful dog to be there sprinting along at his side, but Budweiser was crouched, almost kneeling, with his nose to the ground.

He raced back, only to find the chocolate lab flinching at his touch. "Buddy?" he asked, but the dog merely whined, avoiding his eyes, ears turned down to match his doleful expression. Booger patted his head, splashing fresh rain water, and turned to run off after Eve.

Clearly, this was going to be a solo mission.

Chapter 35

Billy poured Wizzie another glass of her favorite Chianti before topping off his own glass. A soft mandolin played in the background, tuned perfectly in the hands of a little old man on a creaky old stool. The Italian restaurant was small and intimate, just like Billy liked it.

Wizzie looked radiant in the candlelight, eyes twinkling in tune to its flickering flame and admiring the maroon color of her wine in its glass. "I hate to say it, hon, but it's so nice to get out of that house," she said, shivering. "Is that wrong of me to say, Billy?"

"No, honey," he said, gently covering her hand with his own. "It's good to get out from time to time."

"But Eve?" she asked, peering out the window next to their cozy little table for two. "Do you think she's okay?"

Billy turned to follow her gaze. The sky was clear, not a cloud in sight. A full moon shone on a crowded parking lot, dry gravel underneath. There wasn't a breeze to stir the tall pines on either side of the building, nor an ounce of rain to dot the gravel underfoot. In fact, it was the prettiest night they'd seen in a long, long time.

The mandolin player paused between songs and both Wizzie and Billy strained their ears at the window, listening for distant thunder, their eyes ever alert for the flickering fingers of lightning to dance across the peaceful sky.

When a new song started, Billy turned and winked at Wizzie. "Honey, first sign of rain we'll dash out of here, even if it means bolting on our dinners—and the check! But until then…" He watched her smile, reassured by his calming voice and soothing words. "This is our night. Eve said so herself."

"But wasn't she just being polite?" Wizzie fretted, taking a sip from her glass before putting it back down.

Billy took a bite out of a breadstick and chuckled. "Did you see how that gal was dressed when we left? Honey, she wasn't going anywhere. Shoot, she was probably relieved to get out from under our feet for a few hours."

Wizzie laughed, finally picking up a breadstick of her own. She'd lost weight since the first signs of haunting, and he was happy to see her nibbling the long white stick now.

"She always was an independent one," Wizzie recalled fondly. "I think you're right; a little time away from us, from me, is all that girl needs to feel shipshape."

"Well, that and hightailing it out of that haunted house first thing in the morning," Billy added, sipping his wine. It was a little too sweet for his taste, but it didn't matter; Wizzie usually polished off the bottle for the both of them. It was her one indulgence, and Billy was just glad to see her happy again, smiling, laughing…eating!

The waiter brought their salads and Billy looked out over the crowded restaurant. It was a random weeknight in Mystery Acres. Raddicio's was the only decent joint in town and always packed a hearty crowd, day or night.

The faces at the other tables all looked so happy and carefree. Billy wondered what it might be like to go out to dinner, eat your meal, pay your check, drive home and not be filled with dread to open your front door.

He wondered idly if Chief Running Blood would always be with them, how often they'd see the glowing red wolf, or the Indian brave who offered help, only to vanish into the night, never to return.

He wondered if life would always be like this, hard work and long nights spent worrying about Wizzie, always expecting a phone call every time a candle blew out or a window slammed shut or rain fell.

Wizzie cleared her throat and he turned to find her, salad fork halfway to her lips. "Penny for your thoughts?" she said sweetly, and the last thing Billy wanted to do was worry her tonight.

Not tonight.

He chuckled and dug into his salad. "I was wondering where that waiter went off to with his fancy pepper grinder."

They chuckled and tried to avoid looking out the window for signs of rain. And even when they did, there wasn't a cloud, or a ripple in the tree branches, or a drop on the parking lot gravel.

All was right in the world. For this one, peaceful night, they could stop worrying, enjoy their wine, and each other. Billy sighed, staring down at his empty salad plate.

If only he could believe that.

Chapter 36

Eve stumbled onto the bridge, bare feet slippery on the slick wooden slats beneath her as she flailed her arms wildly. The stinging rain was blinding as her right hand struggled to find the wet railing.

She clung to it desperately as the tiny bridge tossed and turned in the swirling winds, feeling no more substantial than a tissue in a flushing toilet.

The wind howled all around her, in front of her, to her left, at her back, to her right, almost—but not quite—drowning out the chanting curses of the glowing red Indian chief at her back.

He stood, one foot on the bridge, the other on the riverbank, waving a glowing stick and chanting, eyes closed. His words grew more powerful and persistent with every step she took in the opposite direction.

Not that she could go far. The rain pounded, the wind howled and now the waves lapped over the sides of the bridge, the river having risen several inches, maybe even feet, since she began running toward the safety of the bridge only minutes earlier.

She pulled herself along, hands bone white on the wet wooden railing as her feet danced out from beneath her, threatening to send her into the raging Wolf Creek any second.

Eve whimpered, on the verge of tears but too busy trying to survive to cry. The bridge had seemed but a small span to cross moments earlier but now, half-blinded by the storm, with heavy clouds blotting out the moon and water crashing over and through the boards beneath her feet, it seemed like miles until she reached the other side.

She slipped, momentarily grabbing the small railing to keep herself from falling into the raging river beneath her feet, but barely. Hanging by the crook of her arm, she wiped her ruined hair out of her stinging eyes with her free hand, and stared back at the shoreline.

Despite all her running, slipping and sliding, trembling and moaning, she'd hardly gone five feet from the muddy, sodden shores. The chief was there chanting, his strong arms rising in the wind. As if he knew she was watching him, his eyes opened, glowing hot coal red. He smirked, cast his arms in her direction and, as if by magic, waves splashed over the bridge, nearly carrying her away.

She felt her arm strain as she struggled to rise and keep going, and knew that it would be sore tomorrow. If she made it to tomorrow. Eve resolved to do just that. She struggled to her feet, despite the storm seeming to intensify with every step.

She inched forward with both hands on the rail, her feet sliding out from beneath her as if in a wind tunnel. One step, two slips, one step, three slips, fall, and still somehow she made it to the middle of the creaking, sagging bridge.

She stood as tall as she could, struggling to catch her breath. Though she'd only managed to go a few feet, Eve felt as if she'd just finished a 5K run in record time. The wind bent her back down, forcing her to curl almost into a ball even as she clung to the wet, slippery railing with all her might.

In the distance she could hear a new sound. She stood a little taller, bracing herself against the howling wind and stinging rain, and peered out into the distance where, to her horror, Eve saw something she would have never imagined in little Wolf Creek: a massive wave, crested and white, rolling toward her at a blinding speed.

She shrieked, though the sound was quickly stolen by the fierce, howling wind, and stumbled along, letting go of the rail in favor of speeding her progress.

It proved a fatal mistake, for the minute she did, the wind howled, swirling around Eve, forcing her back against the other side of the railing as the bridge sagged, creaked and succumbed to the massive wave that broke over it.

She fell back into the water, the frigid cold taking her breath even as the surging waves filled her mouth and lungs with brackish, cold water.

She gasped and gulped but it was no use. There was nothing left to cling to, no rocks or railing or shore, only the rushing wave that sent her swirling through the cold darkness, taking her down and away to where Eve knew there would be no return.

Chapter 37

Booger watched helplessly as the chief guarded the footpath to the bridge. He clung to a wet tree, trying to stand upright as the wind knocked him back down to his knees. He sank in the mud, struggling to keep his eyes open as the chief chanted, waving and rattling his bone stick in the hoarse, blinding wind.

Booger watched poor Eve limp farther onto the bridge, her robe in tatters, her hair covering her eyes, her skin pale in the damp, dark air as the wind tossed and turned her this way and that.

She said not a word as she struggled alone, and he desperately wanted to reach out to her, to race past the chief, call out to her and scream support. But he dared not; the chief was so close, glowing red, seven feet tall, giant and deadly that Booger feared if he said one word or moved one inch Chief Running Blood would turn his rage on him as well.

He looked behind him, thinking perhaps he might be able to run back along the waterline and get across Wolf Creek some other way, but it was miles to the Fulsom Bridge, and in this weather it would take over an hour, maybe longer.

He shook his head and watched silently as Eve stumbled across the bridge. Not that she made much progress. Every step seemed to take forever, and even then she was as likely to slip, trip or be blown off her feet as soon as she tried to put her bare foot down on the slippery wood beneath her.

The wind howled and Booger found it easier if he looked away, squinting if not closing his eyes altogether against the driving rain. He shivered in his shorts and T-shirt, the temperature having dropped nearly ten degrees, maybe more, since he'd slipped from his room and found the Franks' porch damaged by the storm.

Booger heard Chief Running Blood chanting amid the driving rain and crackling thunder, but he couldn't make out the words and didn't dare try to get a closer look by reading his lips.

Instead he cowered, feeling helpless and shamed as Eve cried out. His heart pounded with every step she took, fearing for her life as the creek swelled and the waves grew higher and higher, white caps splashing down into themselves, spraying him with cold, salty water as he clung to his young sapling with all his might.

The ground beneath him grew wet and soggy, and his knees sank deeper into the cold, clingy mud. Chief Running Blood murmured and muttered, shaking his glowing red bone stick, raising his arms as the storm intensified. The rain seemed to blow harder, wetter, faster and colder with every word.

The gale took his breath away, and he was on shore. Booger could only imagine how Eve felt, clinging for all her life to the wet, soggy railing of the trembling little bridge. She wasn't even halfway across it when Booger heard the hard, fast rumbling of a wall of water, a massive wave, coming her way.

"No!" he cried, struggling to stand, but the mud had Booger in its grip and wouldn't let go. His feet were stuck even as he dragged himself up from his knees using the tree's young branches for support. "Eve!" he shouted, Chief Running Blood be damned. "No, come back!"

But she couldn't hear. Even the chief himself ignored Booger, chanting still, raising his arms as if he had control of the very river itself. In response, the wave grew and grew, faster and faster, barreling right for Eve—then through her, and over her.

She disappeared in a wall of white water without a sound, alone, and Booger found himself rushing away from the tree, suddenly freed. He bounded toward the water's edge, stumbling heavily in the still blinding rain with shoes full of mud. When he reached the bridge —or where the bridge had been a few moments earlier—Chief Running Blood was no longer there.

Booger stood, the water rushing over his feet even though he was still on land. The bridge was completely gone, the rapids raging, and Eve was nowhere to be seen.

As the rain subsided and the water calmed, Booger fell to his knees, watching closely but finding nothing, not a trace of her. He waded into the water, which was suddenly calm. The clouds parted and moonlight shone down on the placid water, as if the rain still dripping from Booger's face had all been merely part of his imagination.

"Eve?" he asked no one as the night sky sat, silent, dark and heavy above. "Eve?"

The water lapped gently around his feet, the bridge completely gone, washed away, as if it had never been there at all. He stood, tired, soaked, uncertain and anxious, then sank to his knees and cried as all around him, as if in mourning, the crickets chirped once more.

Chapter 38

Wizzie was nervous as they drove home, despite the lovely dinner and extra glass of wine she'd had with dessert. Billy held her hand as they wound through Mystery Acres' quiet city streets.

"They sure do button up early around here." He sighed contentedly, her head upon his shoulder as they shared his half of the truck's large bench seat.

"Lucky for us our dancing days are through," Wizzie mumbled, tired beyond description but unreasonably wired. She often felt like that these days; numb from lack of sleep, but too awake to consider napping or sleeping any longer when her eyes popped open in the middle of the night.

"Hey," he chuckled, nudging her gently with a twitch of his broad shoulder. "Speak for yourself."

"You know what I mean," she said, pushing gently away from him so she could study his still handsome face. "I just...I keep waiting for my joy to come back, Billy."

He nodded, understanding written upon every line of his face. "I'm trying to bring it back to life, sweetheart," he said, gently patting her thigh. "Like tonight. Wasn't dinner out nice?"

She smiled, nodding. "We haven't done that in so long," she said. "I loved every minute…"

"But?" he asked, as if sensing it in her voice.

She shrugged; she never could hide her emotions from him. "But now it's over and we have to go home."

He chuckled. "I know, Baby Dolly, but where do you want to go? Some no-tell motel?"

She was still chuckling when they turned down Foxtrot Lane, a sudden downpour taking visibility from one hundred percent down to less than ten.

"What the—?" Billy grumbled as he slowed to a crawl, hitting the windshield wipers and peering through the glass. "Where did this come from?"

Wizzie gripped the doorframe as the rain battered the truck, the wind whirling outside her window and rocking the cab as Billy pumped the brakes.

"I can't see anything," he mumbled, but she did.

There, beyond the cul-de-sac, was a glowing figure, red, massive and shaking something in his muscular arm. "I do," she murmured and, before she could help herself, she slipped from the truck.

"Eve!" she called out, stumbling through the rain to reach their front stoop. The wood was saturated, as if it had been raining for some time. She slid up the steps, wind howling, only to open the door and find the house deserted. "Eve!" she called, running through the foyer and noting the smell of fresh coffee as she was drawn inevitably toward the back porch.

"Wizzie!" Billy shouted, stumbling through the front door. But she ignored him, tearing through the slider only to find the porch a wreck, the wind whipping cushions onto the lawn and candles rolling around under her feet. She stumbled and fell on the slick wood and winced when she scraped her knee as she slid toward the steps.

Thunder cracked and the wind howled and she was blown back against a fallen deck chair, its legs poking into her back as Billy stumbled to the sliding glass door.

"Get in here!" he shouted, voice nearly stolen by the harsh wind.

"I can't," she said, pulling herself to her knees. "I can't find Eve!"

"I'm sure she's here somewhere," Billy mumbled at her back, or perhaps he was shouting and simply couldn't be heard above the shrieking wind.

"Booger?" Wizzie asked, spotting a small figure clinging to a young sapling along the water's edge. She stood and leaned against the porch railing as Billy stumbled out to join her. "Booger!"

She called out, but she might as well have been using sign language. The rushing wind stole her words and threw them back at her, along with a sheet of stinging rain and a gust of frozen wind that sent her and Billy back down to their knees.

"Why is Booger out there?" she asked, clinging to the porch railing as Billy held up a ruined seat cushion to shelter them.

"Why are *we* out here?" Billy asked, trying to drag her back inside.

She stood, nodding, and turned, when the glow of Chief Running Blood caught her eye. She ripped herself from Billy's arms and, using the porch railing, dragged herself to the farthest corner of the porch and leaned over, watching as the chief waved his bone stick and his arms, appearing to control the very storm itself.

But it wasn't the chief she was interested in, it was the figure just beyond him, quivering, stuck, clinging to the middle of the tiny wooden bridge that spanned Wolf Creek and led to the golf course across the street.

"Eve!" she shouted just as thunder roared and lightning cracked and the rushing sound of an approaching wave sent chills through her body. But that was impossible; this was Wolf Creek, not the Pacific Ocean!

"Eve!" Wizzie shouted once more. The wave crested, a tidal wave of white foam and roaring water bearing straight down, then over, the tiny bridge. "EVE!"

Wizzie burst from the porch and stumbled to the soft, muddy ground below. The storm still raged, water surging, stilling her progress as she floundered. Billy was there at her side, holding her back as she struggled against him.

"Wizzie," he said, pulling her tight. "She's gone, she's gone..."

Wizzie turned and pushed him away, struggling as she watched Booger stumble to the shoreline and sink knee-deep into the water as he looked at where the bridge had just been.

"Eve!" he called out to no avail, and as the storm subsided and the rain suddenly halted, she saw why: Chief Running Blood was gone, as if he'd never been there at all.

Chapter 39

Booger sat on the banks of Wolf Creek, picking blades of grass out of the ground with a pale, trembling hand. Budweiser lay on his other side, snout on his paws, whimpering every few minutes as if he, too, was in mourning.

His poor mom, always exhausted, was so worried about him that she took off a couple of days from work to sit with him. She was also in shock. She grew up around this area close to the Alabama River and had heard stories as a child but she never knew such a thing could really happen. It was horrible.

Booger was tired; tired of not sleeping, of not eating, of not laughing or smiling. About all he could do was cry late at night when his room was dark, with his eyes wide open, the thoughts and fears and dark ghosts coming to haunt him all over again.

As soon as daylight came, he would crawl from his window and bathe in it, letting the warm rays dance across his pale face and the bags under his eyes, drying them in the sun. He was glad to be out of his dark, claustrophobic room, where even the shadows threatened him.

Now the sun was high and with it came activity far beyond the rows of small saplings that dotted the riverbanks. It had only been a few days since the freak storm that killed Wizzie's sister, and already the county had big trucks and rigs and dozens of workers wading in the river—now as calm and tranquil as glass—erecting a new bridge.

Booger watched them stumbling around in big wading boots, laughing to each other. They were just workmen on a crew, ball caps and beards and sunburns and no idea that a few nights earlier a beautiful young woman had struggled for her life—and lost it—on the spot where they spat tobacco and scratched under their arms.

He sighed, turned away, and stared down into the dirt at his feet. If only he didn't feel so alone. But he was; it couldn't be helped. Wizzie and Billy were back in Decatur attending Eve's funeral, leaving Booger to mourn alone in his own way.

For him, that meant sitting on the bank, knees against his chest, arms on top of his knees, staring at the placid water, absentmindedly tearing clumps of grass with his left hand.

He had barely slept since the storm, and doubted he'd ever have another good night's sleep for the rest of his life. Booger had never known anyone who'd died before.

Well, that wasn't entirely true: his grandfather had died when Booger was just a kid, but he'd hardly known the man and now he was able to visit Grandma in the nursing home twice a month. So it wasn't really the same. And besides, Grandpa had been really old by all accounts and, had lived a long, full, rich life.

But Eve was young, too young to die. She had her whole life ahead of her. That is, until Chief Running Blood decided that she was the enemy.

Booger shivered at the thought of the chief's awesome power. The chief hadn't just done a little rain dance and made it sprinkle; he had literally created a killer storm. If he could do that to poor Eve, who didn't even live here, what did he have in store for Wizzie and Billy and himself?

Booger's stomach clenched, reminding him he hadn't eaten since the day before. He couldn't help it; he just didn't have any appetite. He was constantly nervous, wondering when Chief Running Blood would strike next.

Budweiser whined plaintively, and Booger smiled, turning to look down at his faithful dog. He took his right hand from his knee and patted his old pal, whose dark brown fur was warm in the lazy Alabama sun.

"I know what you mean, boy," he said, voice hoarse from the crying he did late at night when he was unable to sleep and the world grew dark and the walls closed in. "I know exactly what you mean."

Chapter 40

Wizzie sat slumped against the passenger door, still in her black dress from Eve's funeral. On the seat between them was a care package, stuffed with plastic containers brimming with leftovers from the wake.

They sat untouched, just like Wizzie's plate after the service.

"You've got to eat sometime," Billy reminded her gently as he patted her hand. She flinched at his touch. Not because it was unwelcome, but because she'd been lost in her own world again.

"I will," she lied. Wizzie doubted she'd ever eat again.

"I'll feed you in your sleep if you don't," Billy said.

She turned to him, so handsome in his black funeral suit with the crisp white shirt and thin black tie. "Good luck getting me to sleep." She sighed, turning to stare back out the window before he could see her crying again.

They drove in silence for a while, the day still young on account of her leaving the wake early. "You sure you're not going to regret not staying longer?" he asked after a few minutes.

She sighed again, voice steady enough to speak once more. "I just couldn't stay a minute longer," she confessed, turning to face him. "Do you think they'll forgive me?"

"Baby Dolly," he said, smirking. "My daddy had a saying: never blame people for what they do at weddings and funerals—they're temporarily insane."

Wizzie smiled as much as she could. "That's true enough," she said, staring at the endless ribbon of county asphalt stretching out for miles in front of them. "I just don't feel myself, hon."

"Nor will you for quite some time, I expect."

She nodded. Billy could always make her feel better. Not good, in this case, but better.

"I just can't help but thinking it was our fault, Billy," she confessed, voice breaking. "And I should have known. Billy, when I was at the cemetery in Decatur a few months back, a magpie flew right over me and his mate never came. Don't you see? My family's cursed. Two generations died seven years apart and now Eve is the third generation to die in seven years again."

"Honey," he said with a powerful sigh. Wizzie knew she sounded like a broken record; she just couldn't help it.

"I do, Billy," she sputtered, the waterworks starting all over again. "We invited her down and acted like nothing was wrong. We knew better..."

"Now you stop that, sweet thing," he cooed, hand tightly gripping hers. "Things weren't wrong when Eve came, and they weren't wrong until that last night. And I don't believe about magpies or curses. You know we would have never put her in danger if—"

"I know." Wizzie gasped, blotting her eyes with a used tissue from her purse. "I know, but...my heart tells me different, Billy. The heart don't lie."

Billy turned to her, knowing the road was clear ahead and there was sparse traffic in their lane. "It does when you're grieving, darling. It lies all the durn time."

She nodded, but only to hush him up. She needed time alone, time to think, although she desperately wanted Billy's warm body on the seat next to her.

"Lily looked really good," Billy commented softly. "She wanted to come home with us."

"I know and I told her absolutely not." Wizzie cried. "She wouldn't be safe there."

Her heart ached with loss, and she knew she'd never forgive herself for letting Eve come to her...her...haunted house. "What do we do now, Billy?" she fretted, staring out the window as the trees flew by.

"Honey," he sighed, fingers gripped tight around the wheel. "I honestly don't know."

"Me either," she confessed. "I just...how long can we ride this roller coaster?"

"Maybe...maybe he's done with us," Billy mused, and they both knew there was no need to mention who "he" was.

"We thought that last time, Billy," she reminded him. "And now we're coming back from a funeral."

He nodded and pushed his tongue against his lower lip, a thing he did when thinking too hard for too long. "I don't know what else to do." He sighed. "I'm up for a promotion at work, we're going into our busy season, you've made that house so pretty..."

"I don't want to leave either," she confessed, earning wide eyes and arched eyebrows from her handsome husband. "Fact is I want to stay more than ever, if only to see that Chief Running Blood bleeds for real."

"You mean that?" he asked.

"I think so," she said, looking over at him. "I think...I think now we have to see this through to the end, no matter what. Don't you?"

Billy nodded, looking at her simple black dress. "I think we owe it to your sister to make sure no one else suffers the same way."

Wizzie nodded, reaching for his hand. "I think you're right, hon."

Chapter 41

Wizzie felt something in the air the minute they turned down Shady Acres Drive toward their subdivision on Deer Run Ridge. A chill splashed across her body, though the windows were closed and the air had been set at the same setting the whole way back from Decatur.

"Ooooh," she shivered aloud as Billy instinctively slowed the truck down.

"You all right, Baby Dolly?" he asked, slow Southern drawl soft with concern.

"No," she confessed, looking over at him. "I think…I think we have a welcoming party."

As they drove onto Deer Run Ridge, Billy sighed with relief. "Just your boyfriend, Booger," he chuckled, seeing the ninth grader sitting on the front porch, sulking.

"Poor kid." Wizzie sighed, clucking her tongue. "To see Eve go like that. He must be hurting as bad as we are, honey, but at least we have each other."

Billy nodded, easing the car up slowly. Booger looked strange. Pale, unkempt, his clothes wrinkly where they weren't greasy, and greasy where they weren't wrinkled.

His eyes were half-lidded, and he seemed to be sleeping. Billy pulled the truck to a stop and Wizzie got out, closing her door quietly as if not to wake him.

"He's not asleep," Wizzie said as Billy stood by the truck, grabbing their small overnight bags from the truck bed. "He's looking at us."

He was. Booger's head rose slowly, mouth half open, eyes widening. He stood sluggishly, arms and legs looking rubbery, as if they were all asleep.

"Booger?" Billy asked, pausing by the front of the truck.

Booger ignored him, raising his hands. "Be gone," he said, mouth wide open, head thrown back. Wizzie froze right where she was. The voice was not his own. It was deep, cold and ancient. "Be gone," it said again as Booger's arms waved. "Let the death of the white girl be a warning, and walk here no more! Blood, blood, blood. Your death is still to come."

The voice thundered as Booger's arms waved, his head lolling on his shoulders, feet unsteady.

And then he collapsed, sinking to his knees in the gravel.

"Booger!" she cried, rushing to his side.

"No, Wizzie, don't!" Billy cautioned, but she already knew the demon was gone, had fled from here, leaving Booger alone, abandoned, frail.

His skin was clammy as she helped him sit up. He looked dazed, blinking as he mumbled hoarsely, "What…when did you get back?"

"Just now, Booger," she said, calmly. "Don't you remember talking to us?"

He looked at her, eyes widening. "I…where am I?"

"Here," Wizzie said. Billy crouched in the gravel next to her. "At our house."

Booger shook his head. "The last thing I remember, Budweiser and I were down by the creek, watching the men building the new bridge." He looked around wildly. "Where…where is he?"

Wizzie frowned, dread filling her stomach. *Please*, she begged God as they helped Booger to his feet and searched for his beloved chocolate lab. *Please let us find Budweiser safe and sound.*

Toni House

Chapter 42

They searched and searched, but couldn't find Budweiser anywhere. "Budweiser!" Booger shouted.

"Buddy!" called Billy.

"Budweiser, honey," cooed Wizzie, but nothing. None of it worked. Not even a little. It was as if the dog had just vanished. Booger was inconsolable. First what had happened with Eve, and now his best friend gone, missing.

Booger and his mom printed up flyers and posted them all over town but heard nothing.

Booger stumbled around for a day or two, long after Billy and Wizzie had given up the hunt, searching for Budweiser. He was rooting around in the bushes, in a spot he'd searched a dozen times before, when he heard rustling.

"Budweiser?" Booger called, and gasped when he heard a wet, garbled yelp in reply.

"Buddy!" he cried, rushing through the bushes to see Budweiser limping toward him. He sank to his knees and wrapped his arms around Budweiser's neck. He was cold, and slimy, as if he'd been locked in a refrigerator for a month.

Booger knew the poor chocolate lab had been wandering around the riverbed for two long, cold days and stood to lead him home.

"Come on, boy," Booger said, ruffling the matted, greasy coat between Budweiser's shoulder blades. "Let's get you home and safe and dry."

Luckily Booger's mom was at a continuing education class for her nursing job or she would have had a coronary watching him give Budweiser a bath in the guest room tub. But even after half a bottle of shampoo and two bars of soap, Budweiser still looked matted and scraggly when Booger had dried him off and led him into the kitchen for some grub.

Budweiser didn't want his dry food or even his wet food. He yipped and growled at the closed fridge until Booger got the hint and found some raw meat. There was a pound of ground beef Booger was supposed to turn into hamburgers while his mom was away, and the minute he took it out of the fridge Budweiser leapt for it, dragged it out of his hands and tore open the package right there on the linoleum floor.

He chomped and chewed and when Booger reached for the plastic wrapper to throw it away, Budweiser nipped at his hands, growling as his muzzle wrinkled and drooled with white, speckled phlegm.

"Whoa, boy," Booger said, leaving the dog be as he scarfed up the cold, raw hamburger and then licked the floor to snatch up every last crumb. "I forgot you haven't eaten in a few days."

But even as Budweiser limped off to the back porch to lounge in the sun and growl at the riverbank, Booger knew it was more than that. He picked up the phone and dialed Wizzie's number. Billy was at work, as usual, but at least Wizzie might be able to stop by and see if Booger was crazy.

"Wizzie?" he asked, sounding more desperate than he'd intended when she answered. "Can you…do you think you could come over to my house for a second?"

Wizzie didn't hesitate. "I'll be right there, Boog," she said, calling him by the nickname she'd started using lately. He waited, pacing, biding his time between cleaning up the mess Budweiser had left in the tub and the mess he'd left on the kitchen floor.

Booger was just washing his hands when he heard the doorbell ring and he sprang into the foyer, drying them on his pants before he opened the door.

"What's wrong, Boog?" Wizzie asked, seeing the panicked look on his face.

"I…I found Budweiser," he confessed as Wizzie raced inside. But he needn't have bothered. She stopped in her tracks—they both did—to find Budweiser standing in the living room, staring at them, eyes glowing red in the dim interior lighting, muzzle wrinkled in a slow, low growl.

"What's gotten into him?" Wizzie asked, standing next to Booger in the foyer.

"I don't know," Booger practically whimpered, looking up at her. "That's…that's why I called you."

Wizzie nodded, looking from Booger to Budweiser and jutting out her chin. "Okay," she said, as if to herself. "Okay then."

She put on a fixed smile, inching toward Budweiser. "That's a good boy," she said, hand out, but instead of calming down, Budweiser barked, the sound loud and violent and echoing in the tight, enclosed space of the foyer.

"Budweiser!" Booger shouted, rushing to get between them. "Bad dog. Stop!"

Budweiser growled lower, but stopped barking. "I…I'm sorry," Booger gushed, turning toward Wizzie. "He…he's never done that before."

"I know," she gasped, hand clutched at her throat. "Booger, I don't know about this…"

He shook his head, realizing it was a bad idea to get Wizzie involved. "It's okay," he said, scooting her back toward the door. "I shouldn't have bothered you. He's just cold and tired from being lost, that's all. I'll…we'll get a good night's sleep, Wizzie, and we'll try again tomorrow."

Wizzie nodded, smiling toward Budweiser, but dragged Booger onto the porch. "Booger," she scolded, when the screen door had shut behind them. "You don't need me to tell you that Budweiser's just not right."

Booger bit his lower lip, staring at his dirty sneakers. "I know, but what can I do?"

Wizzie shrugged. "Booger, I don't know, but I don't feel it's right you being over here with Budweiser acting like that. Come stay with Billy and me tonight. At least until your mother gets home."

Booger shook his head, resolved. "I can't leave him here like this," he insisted, looking back through the screen door where Budweiser lay, head on his paws, red eyes glowing, watching them. "He'll…he'll be better after a good night's sleep, Wizzie, promise."

But even after Wizzie left, under much protest, Booger wasn't so sure.

Chapter 43

Booger slept with one eye open for as long as he could, but Budweiser slept with two eyes open. They glowed red as coals in the darkness of his room.

He watched them, brooding and silent, until he drifted into sleep. Booger didn't know how long he'd slept, but it couldn't have been very long when an eerie chill woke him with a start.

"Huuummmmphpphfuzzzzleeesnort!" He gasped, sitting up straight in his twisted bed sheets, the room glowing red with Budweiser's eyes peering through the darkness. "Boy?" he asked, rubbing the sleep from his eyes. "What…what is it?"

Booger stumbled from his sheets, realizing he'd been so tired from watching Budweiser growl all day he'd fallen asleep in his clothes. Even his shoes!

Budweiser stood on his hind legs, paws on the windowsill, growling at a shape outside in the dark. Booger stood from the bed and went to pat Budweiser's head. The dog turned, growling, eyes bright red, lips bared, teeth white and shocking in the dark.

Booger flinched and stumbled back through the room toward the door. Budweiser turned back to the window, ignoring Booger. The room was cold. Booger clutched his arms as he grabbed the doorknob and, for the first time in his young life, shut—and locked—the door against his own beloved dog.

Budweiser knew it immediately and wailed and keened, heavy paws padding against the hardwood floor as he threw himself at the door Booger had just closed. It bent outward as Booger stumbled back into the hallway and rushed for the patio doors.

The whole house was cold, as if frost had covered the living room furniture and crept up the walls. He shivered and burst onto the patio, the warm Alabama air soft on his skin. He panted, stomach clenched and sore, as he crept down the wooden porch steps until his sneakers pressed into the damp, dewy grass.

But he wasn't alone. There, on the lawn just outside his bedroom window, stood the wolf. The red wolf. But for once Booger wasn't afraid. The wolf looked at him, eyes red but also sad. His face was calm, almost placid, glowing softly in the middle of the night.

It nodded toward him, opening its soft muzzle to speak, so tall Booger had to look up, straining his neck, to see it all. The night was peaceful, calm, except for the vicious dog barking in Booger's room. Booger shook his head, whimpering softly, but the wolf merely nodded, looking back through the window.

As if on cue, Budweiser crashed against the glass, cracking it as Booger stumbled to his knees. The wolf growled, giant teeth bared, shoulders hunched, glistening red hair on edge as Budweiser sailed back against the window, cracking it some more, until a shard of glass popped out and fell at the wolf's front paws.

The wolf growled, leaning down and inching back, as Budweiser leapt through the bedroom window, glass shattering and blowing outward as if something had just exploded inside.

Booger gasped and stumbled backward as Budweiser landed on his feet, growling, gnashing his teeth at the wolf and sprinting straight toward Booger.

"Budweiser!" he screamed. "No, boy, it's me! Booger!"

But it was no use. Budweiser was tearing along the grass, snout open, teeth bared, speckled hot drool flying in white foamy waves from his lips. Booger turned and ran but it was no use. Budweiser would be on him in seconds, tearing him to pieces.

His own dog!

Is this how Eve felt? Booger wondered as he stumbled and fell to his knees as the chill of Budweiser's greasy dark brown coat crept toward him. Cold and alone and scared, with no one to save him?

There was a vicious growl and much upturning of earth, and a sad, scared little yelp.

Booger turned, wanting Budweiser's face to be the last thing he saw, but it wasn't. The wolf had him, teeth bared into Budweiser's side, shaking him like a rag doll before releasing him. He tossed Budweiser to the ground and stood over him triumphantly.

Booger didn't know what to do. Was he next? Would the wolf tear him to bits as well? Or would Budweiser rise from the dirt, growling, and skin him alive instead?

In the end, neither happened. The wolf approached, and Booger scrambled back, back, until his shoulders came square against the porch steps and he had nowhere else to go.

The wolf's eyes glowed, his mouth opened and, softly, the beast leaned down and licked Booger's face. It was cold and warm at the same time, soft and hard, like the skin of a shark. Booger whimpered, helpless, defenseless, until the wolf turned and, with great paws loping through the grass, trotted off and disappeared in a shower of bleak, cold mist.

Booger panted, collapsing into himself, rolling onto his side and staring at Budweiser as the dog writhed in the dirt. "Budweiser?" he asked, rising to his knees and crawling to his beloved pet. "Buddy?"

The dog rolled over, wet and muddy, eyes soft and brown like before he'd gone missing. "Budweiser?" The chocolate lab trembled, rising to all four legs and limping over to Booger with his tongue hanging out.

Booger was worried, afraid about what might happen, but he needn't have. Instead of tearing him limb from limb, Budweiser fell into his lap, panting, wet, ragged, but not bloodied. He whimpered, licking Booger's hands as they both lay there panting, damp with early morning dew, under a blanket of stars, both of them grateful for the other.

But Booger had someone—or something—else to be grateful for as well: the wolf. He couldn't wait to tell Wizzie and Billy what had happened. That is, just as soon as Budweiser was rested and could follow him to their house.

Chapter 44

Booger waited until the next night to tell Wizzie about Budweiser. Billy was at work, training his replacement for the graveyard shift, and when she heard Budweiser panting in the bushes beyond her porch, Wizzie stood frightened with a hand at her throat.

"It's okay," Booger said, smiling and patting Budweiser on the head. "I have a story to tell you, and Bud here is my proof."

"Are you sure?" she asked, still closer to bolting through the sliding glass doors at her back than sitting down with him on the cozy porch.

"I promise, Wizzie," Booger said. "Honest, Budweiser's all better."

"But how?" she asked, finally sitting back down. Without any prompting, Budweiser loped over to her and promptly licked her hand. That was all it took to put Wizzie's fears to rest. She patted his head and ruffled his ears and made baby cooing noises that made Booger wince.

"How did this happen?" she asked, looking up as Booger slid into the seat across from her.

"The wolf did it," he explained excitedly, on the edge of his deck chair just thinking about it.

"The red wolf?" Wizzie asked.

He nodded. "She saved my life!"

"Budweiser?" she asked.

"No, the red wolf. Budweiser was going to chow down on me when all of a sudden, the red wolf showed up and saved me."

Wizzie shook her head. "So the red wolf is a *good* ghost?"

Booger nodded. "She is for Budweiser. If she hadn't come along when she did, Buddy here might have, well..."

As if he knew what Booger was saying, Budweiser loped back over from Wizzie's chair and laid his head on Booger's lap. Booger patted his head absently while Wizzie shook hers.

"I just want it all to stop," she said softly.

Booger nodded. "Me, too, Wizzie, but how?"

"I want to think Chief Running Blood has gone away," she said. "But then, who else could have done that to Budweiser?"

Booger shook his head. The night was dark. And then, suddenly it wasn't.

"Booger?" Wizzie asked as she stood, pointing over his shoulder. He turned and smiled, seeing the red wolf rise from the riverbank and stand proudly just beyond the porch.

"It's okay," he said hopefully, but his voice was a little shaky.

"Come over here just the same," Wizzie said, sounding just like Booger's mother. He did, slinking across the porch until she stood in front of him protectively.

The red wolf glowed, massive and bright, eyes watching them carefully.

"Who are you?" Wizzie asked, startling Booger with her volume —and her tone. "What do you want?"

The red wolf bowed her head almost to the grass beyond Wizzie's porch and made a soft keening sound, as if trying to talk.

"Are…are you friendly?" Booger asked, and the red wolf raised her head in a questioning nod.

Then, from the trees, emerged another figure, the ghostly brave. Booger gasped and Wizzie tried to yank him back behind her again, but he was having none of it.

"We want to protect you," said the brave in a voice so cold and dark Booger did shrink back by Wizzie's side. At least, just a little. "That is why we remain here."

Booger inched out from beside Wizzie and studied the brave. He was tall, a giant, glowing a softer red than the wolf but still bright. He looked young, even in his spiritual glow. Older than Booger by years, but younger than Wizzie or Billy.

"Who are you?" Wizzie asked, a catch in her throat.

"I am Red Wolf," said the brave, and Booger noticed whenever the brave spoke his appearance blurred and wavered, as if it took too much power to stand in front of them and speak at the same time. "This is Tala, my constant companion."

Booger cocked his head. "But shouldn't *she* be Red Wolf?"

The brave smiled. "In my language, Tala means wolf. Since she was my companion in life, my tribe named me 'Red Wolf' in her honor. Much has changed since our time."

"How…how did you die?" Wizzie asked, a sad note to her tone.

Red Wolf seemed to glow with rage and, in its wake, the very air grew chilled. Booger shivered and Wizzie clasped her arms around her chest.

"Chief Running Blood," was all he said, but it was a mouthful.

"And now?" Wizzie asked. "The chief is back to drive us off his land?"

"Back?" asked the brave, who was bare-chested and wearing leather breeches with an ornate design. "He never left. None of us have. We were cursed since death to roam our land, he to destroy it, Tala and I to protect it."

Red Wolf was growing weak, his image flickering the more he spoke, and even when he didn't, it looked softer, less defined. "I must go," he said, as if reading Booger's mind.

"But how...how can we call on you again?" Wizzie asked, inching past Booger to the edge of the porch. Red Wolf had turned and, next to him, Tala clung protectively.

"We are never far," Red Wolf said before his body disappeared in a burst of soft, red mist. Seconds later, Tala joined him. "We are your protectors," Red Wolf said, voice scattered on the soft Alabama breeze. "Fear no more."

Chapter 45

Wizzie felt the sunlight on her face as she stepped out of the car. It was late afternoon, and she had made a rare trip into town. Not to run errands or pick up milk or bread or mail a letter, but just to get out of the house and see what life was like beyond Wolf Creek. And to pick up the digital camera she'd ordered. She wanted to take pictures of the house and all the decorations she'd made and put them on Facebook and Tumblr and Pinterest.

The town of Camden was picture book on this sunny fall day, and for once she felt well-rested after a good night's sleep that involved no chanting chiefs, no glowing wolves, no talking braves.

She still wore black, in honor of Eve, but for once her mood felt light and she didn't think her sister would mind a day off from the constant grind of fear, anxiety and worry.

She had parked in front of the Sassafras Soda Shoppe, an old time ice cream parlor on Wainscot Way, and sauntered inside for something sweet and cold.

The counter was mostly empty, and she sat toward the end, smiling at the other patrons but remaining cool and distant. She and Billy hadn't socialized much since they'd moved to town. Part of it had been that they were just fine on their own and enjoyed each other's company so much they didn't need a whole cast of characters in their life.

The other part, Wizzie knew, was just plain fear. She had been afraid of leaving the house, of coming home to the house, of staying in the house, of sleeping in the house, of waking in the house. So afraid she just stayed put.

But the night before had been a revelation. Standing there with Booger, staring at two ghosts who called themselves "protectors," a sense of calm had finally come over her.

She had wished Booger good night, watched him walk all the way home, then blew out the candles on the porch, walked upstairs and went straight to bed. That had been before nine at night. She hadn't gotten up until nine the next morning.

It was the longest, the best, the most peaceful sleep she'd had since moving to Mystery Acres and now she felt like celebrating.

"What'll it be, missie?" asked the old timer behind the bar. His nametag read "Gramps" and he had on a stiff paper cap.

"Oh, one root beer float," she said, watching Gramps smile.

"Coming right up," he said, raising a single, withered finger.

She grew calmer still just watching him scoop up the homemade vanilla ice cream into a frosted mug then pour the fresh root beer from a small, thin tap.

"Enjoy," he said, sliding it across to her.

She did, smiling as she savored the midafternoon treat. As she drank, the other diners drifted away. Only one woman at the end of the lunch counter remained: a blonde, frosty, pretty, and familiar looking.

Then Wizzie remembered: their realtor.

"Carol?" she asked, sliding her empty mug away. "Carol Washburn?"

The woman turned, smiling. "Yes?" she asked, face screwing up a little as she tried to remember Wizzie. "Oh, I sold you the old Tanner house."

"Yes," Wizzie said, pulling out a five dollar bill to pay for her float. "How have you been?"

Carol smiled, standing. "I've been well," she said, walking toward Wizzie. "And how about you and that handsome hubby of yours?"

Wizzie was taken aback. Carol Washburn was in her fifties, pretty, blond, leggy, but with a big wedding ring on her finger. And her voice sounded strange. Deeper, colder.

"I-I beg your pardon?" Wizzie stammered, inching back on her counter stool.

"You didn't see how he was looking at me?" she asked. Barked is more like it, her voice turning gruff and unkind.

Wizzie turned, looking to see if Gramps might understand this sudden turn of events, but he had disappeared, off to the stockroom for more whipped cream or waffle cones, she guessed.

"I think you're mistaken," Wizzie said, standing. Or trying to— Carol pushed her back down hard onto the stool.

"Sit there and cower when I talk to you," Carol thundered, voice no longer her own. Wizzie trembled, for she recognized it as Chief Running Blood's.

"No," she whimpered, shaking her head, troubling the hem of her pretty A-line skirt. "No, no, no, no…"

"My patience wears thin," Carol thundered, shaking Wizzie's lapels. "Leave now or I will not be responsible for how many other people die because of you!"

"Because of *you!*" Wizzie screamed back, bolting off her stool and shoving the realtor away from her.

Carol screamed in Chief Running Blood's voice just as Gramps burst from the back room, paper hat crooked on his bald head.

"What in tarnation?" he asked, but it was too late.

As if on cue, Carol slumped to the ground, pale as a scoop of vanilla ice cream, trembling from the cold that had just inhabited her.

"What happened to her?" asked Gramps, reaching for the phone.

"She must have had some kind of fit," Wizzie lied, softly rubbing Carol's hand. It was cold and pale, clammy to the touch. "Are you calling an ambulance?"

"Yes, yes," Gramps wheezed, turning the dial of an old rotary phone. "My goodness."

Carol's eyes flickered open, pale and red, as she blinked. "W-Wizzie?" she asked, shaking her head. "What in tarnation are you doing here?"

"I've been here," Wizzie said, helping her up. "Don't you remember talking to me?"

Carol moaned, holding her head. There was a glass of water on the counter, cold and sweating. Wizzie grabbed it and handed it to her. The realtor gulped it down and gasped. "I-I feel so cold."

Wizzie nodded and slumped down on the floor next to her. From outside in the distance, a siren wailed, and Wizzie knew that Carol would be okay.

If only someone would come and rescue her from this terrible nightmare as well.

Chapter 46

Billy walked out of his supervisor's office with a jaunt in his step, but waited until he turned the corner on the way out to the employee parking lot to breathe.

He could hardly believe his good fortune and kept waiting for someone to step out of the shadows and tell him he was being "punked." He sat in his truck and, with trembling fingers, opened the envelope containing his promotion bonus.

From graveyard shift to night guard Billy had finally been promoted to head of security, meaning regular daylight hours, a full salary—no more clocking in for him each night—and a bonus, his first ever, which his boss had just handed him.

He stared at the check for a long time, heart pounding. Two thousand five hundred dollars. It was more than his take-home pay for two weeks, right there, in his hands, just for getting the top job.

It was still early afternoon and Billy fired up his truck to race to the bank and deposit the check first thing, minus two hundred dollars. He swung by the grocery store and picked up some steaks, potatoes, a nice bottle of red wine and some charcoal, then grabbed fresh flowers on his way to the cash register.

He arrived home, but didn't see Wizzie's car in the drive. He checked his watch, but didn't really have to. The sun was nearly down and Wizzie hated driving in the dark. Why would she be out so late?

He parked the truck and brought the groceries inside, where he chilled the steaks, put the flowers in water and unpacked. There was no note in Wizzie's usual places: taped under a banana magnet on the fridge or next to the phone.

He paced a little, up and down the stairs, in and out of every room, knowing he was being irrational but…really? With all that had been going on lately, giant glowing Indian chiefs and red wolves and warrior braves and Eve's tragic death, what was rational and what wasn't?

He found himself back downstairs, pacing the living room. He wished he had placed one of those GPS tracking devices on her car even though she absolutely forbade it.

At least then he'd know where she was.

The night grew still and dark outside the patio windows, which gave Billy his own concerned reflection back as the lights inside the house turned them into mirrors.

Distressed by the concern on his own face, he turned the lights off, standing in the dark and silence so he could hear Wizzie's car when she finally pulled up.

As he stood then paced in the dark, the red glow began on the riverbank. His stomach clenched; it had been so long since he'd seen the ghost of Red Wolf and Tala.

He watched them appear as if from mist swirling around their feet in a cyclone of power and force until, at last, they stood fully formed and he felt compelled to answer them.

He slid the glass door open and walked cautiously onto the deck. The air was cool, and colder every step he drew near to them.

"Beware the spirit of Chief Running Blood," said the brave, holding a glowing red hand up in greeting. "He works in mysterious ways."

Billy wanted to reply, but his chest was tight, his voice frozen.

"Your wife in danger," said the brave, eyes looking particularly human as Billy found the courage to draw nearer at the news.

"What? Where?"

"You must go to town," he said, pointing with his long, ghostly fingers. "Now before too late."

"But…but…" Billy sputtered helplessly, heart hammering in his chest. "You…Wizzie said you were here to protect us."

"There are places we cannot go," said the brave, almost defensively, as if Billy was accusing him. "There are things we cannot do. But Chief Running Blood roams all this land and is more powerful than you know. Go now, and you protect her."

Billy wasted no time in leaving the ghosts behind. He ran from the porch through the living room and out the front doors, pausing only to grab his keys.

He lit into his truck, fired her up and spun around, spitting gravel beneath his big tires on his way back into town. He cruised up and down the streets, pausing when he saw the flashing red lights of an ambulance outside the local ice cream parlor.

He cruised past slowly, surveying the small crowd still left on the streets, when he saw Wizzie's compact car parked at an expired meter. He jerked into a space, the bed of his truck sticking slightly out into traffic, and ran past the meter without dumping in a coin.

Doors slammed on the ambulance as it pulled away from the curb and he yelled after it, imagining the worst. From the ice cream parlor at his back came a familiar voice. "Billy! What's all this shouting about?"

He saw her wrapped in a blue blanket, ran to her, and embraced her with all his might. "What in tarnation?" he asked when at last he let her up for breath.

"How did you find me here?" she asked instead of answering him.

He pulled her farther away from the doorway, outside where fewer people might hear. "Our protectors told me to come downtown," he said through gritted teeth. "Now tell me what happened."

Chapter 47

Wizzie slept in the next morning, drained from her ordeal with the realtor in the ice cream parlor, terrified of the thought of Chief Running Blood running around town "possessing" random strangers to torture her, Billy and Booger.

Billy was gone when she rose, and she smiled through bittersweet tears to see the flowers he'd bought for her the night before. She'd been too tired for a romantic cookout and had gone to bed minutes after walking in the door.

Now she drank heavily of the coffee he had brewed for her and buttered the wheat toast as soon as it popped up in the toaster. She took both to the patio, her favorite spot in the house, and was finally perking up when the phone rang.

She raced to catch it, spilling coffee on her robe as she stumbled from the patio and into the kitchen. "Yes," she said, picking up the phone on the fourth ring.

"Wizzie Frank?" asked a strange voice, southern accent as rich and syrupy as her husband's.

"Yes," Wizzie answered, paranoid. "May I ask who's calling?"

"Why yes, sugar. This is Amelia Honeycutt and I'm head of the Southern Women's Hospitality League."

Wizzie almost gushed with relief. "Oh goodness," she said, slinking into one of the stools arranged along the far edge of the kitchen counter. "That sounds so nice."

"Well, it is," said Amelia. "And I apologize for being so tardy in my invitation, but we would just love to include you in our annual Home Parade next weekend."

"Home Parade?"

"Why yes, it's where a dozen or so houses all host a small event one weekend every season. Now that fall's come back around, we were hoping you wouldn't mind hosting Saturday evening from four to six at your place out on Wolf Creek?"

"Oh my," said Wizzie, noting the disarray of her normally impeccable living room.

Sensing her hesitation, Amelia said, "You don't need to do much but tidy up a bit, provide some seasonal finger foods, a drink, and let folks come in and tour the home. We provide the sign, the notification, the directions, and everything else."

Wizzie's heart pounded to think of what might happen if Chief Running Blood chose to make an appearance, but early evening was too early for him. And the temptation to host folks at her home, something she'd wanted to do ever since she moved in, proved too great.

"I'll do it!" she said.

"That's just grand," squealed Amelia, clapping her hands on the other end of the line. "I'll let the committee know you're on board and someone will be stopping by in the next few days with signage and a few simple pointers on how to host the event. Thanks so much, Wizzie. I can't wait to meet y'all!"

"Me, too," Wizzie said before hanging up, pulse still racing as she thought of all the preparations she had to do to get ready for the event. For a moment in all the hubbub, she even forgot to be afraid.

Chapter 48

Booger scratched his neck for the twelfth time and tried to stretch his itchy new dress shirt collar, to no avail.

"Booger!" snapped Wizzie as she straightened the throw pillows one last time before her guests arrived. "Quit fussin' with that collar!"

"Yeah, boy," joked Billy, scratching his own neck as if he couldn't breathe. "Suffer like the rest of us."

There was no "rest of us," of course, just Booger and Billy dressed in pleated black slacks, squeaky black shoes and stiff white dress shirts buttoned all the way up.

That was Booger's problem. He lived in T-shirts, V-necks, preferably. The only time he ever wore a collared shirt was in church on Christmas Eve and maybe if there was an assembly at school.

But today he and Billy were "catering" Wizzie's Southern Women's Hospitality League home tour, hence the fancy getups. Wizzie had been going nonstop for days, and it showed.

As the afternoon sun shone through the sliding glass doors, the living room looked like something out of a fashion magazine. There were new slipcovers on the couches, and new pillows, and new candles on the coffee tables, all glittery and aglow.

The floor was polished and waxed and polished some more and light jazz music played on a new speaker system hooked up to Wizzie's cell phone. It was like a whole new house, and soon it would be filled with whole new people.

"You both know what to do, right?" Wizzie asked, nervously checking her hair in the living room mirror.

"Yes, ma'am," Billy said, nudging Booger as he stared down at his shiny new black shoes.

"Uh, yeah, sure," Booger muttered, blushing.

"When the ladies get here," Wizzie reminded them anyway, "wait for them to introduce themselves then offer them a refreshment." For emphasis, she pointed to the new picnic table covered in a fine linen tablecloth and boasting rows and rows of various drinks, from punch to champagne to wine to beer to soda.

"Once the ladies all have a refreshment," Wizzie said, pointing to another table, "offer them a snack." Booger eyed the tiny little sandwiches, rolled wafer cookies, fresh fruit and sliced cheeses and felt his stomach rumble.

He'd been there for hours setting up without a break. Now he clung to his fancy silver serving tray and drooled over the table full of expensive snacks.

Just then the doorbell rang and Wizzie gasped, clutching her hand to her throat and turning to answer it.

"Sorry, Booger," Billy said, wearing a hangdog expression. "You know Wizzie's not normally like this, but she's eager to impress, so..."

"I can see that," Booger said, eyeing the fancy new slipcovers, expensive pillows and tables heaped full of fancy treats.

"Yeah," Billy chuckled humorlessly. "Lucky I got that promotion at work or we would have never been able to afford all this!"

A woman bellowed at the door, oversized and double loud. "I'm Amelia Honeycutt," she said, grabbing Wizzie's hand and pumping it furiously before gliding into the foyer without being invited in. "I hope you don't mind if I come a little early and do a quick inspection?"

"Inspection?" Billy chuckled, nudging Booger's shoulder. "I thought I'd done quit the army already!"

"And who are these fine gentlemen?" Amelia Honeycutt asked and, though her face was smiling, Booger got the distinct impression that the woman didn't approve of them.

"This is my husband, Billy," Wizzie said sweetly, hovering around the larger woman like a hummingbird to a bird feeder. "And our neighbor, Booger."

"Booger?" Amelia gasped, turning up her pug nose. "Well, boy, don't say your name and all should be fine. Are these…will they be wearing uniforms?"

"These are our uniforms," Billy blurted as pleasantly as possible, which wasn't very.

Amelia's piggish green eyes narrowed beneath her stiff bonnet of red hair. "No vests?" she asked, turning to Wizzie with a disapproving sneer. "No bow ties?"

Booger watched as Wizzie's face crumpled. "Well," she said, softly, "no one said anything about vests or bow ties."

Amelia huffed and brushed past, inspecting the snack tables and muttering complaints all the while. "I hope the champagne doesn't get flat before the guests arrive," she said. "Are there any vanilla wafers for those of us allergic to chocolate?"

As Wizzie followed the woman around the house, Billy's face grew red. "I have a right mind to pour some chocolate in her flat champagne," he muttered softly, so as not to be overheard, "and see just how allergic she is!"

Booger snorted and Amelia turned a scornful glance their way. She approached, building up steam for another lecture, but the doorbell rang, saving them both.

"Oh goodness," Amelia gasped, instantly turning her frown upside down as she followed Wizzie to the door. "Our guests are here early!"

"Our guests?" Billy asked, and all Booger could do was shake his head. Here Wizzie had been looking forward to this day all week, and now she was just a nervous wreck.

Chapter 49

Wizzie finally reached for a glass of champagne—far from flat!—and sipped it carefully. Darkness had fallen outside her beautiful house and although the Home Parade was supposed to be over by 6 p.m., everyone was having such a good time they had all decided to stay.

Now it was nearly seven, and the snacks were mostly gone as were the drinks. But she couldn't have cared less. She had done it! Despite Amelia Honeycutt's meddling and doom and gloom attitude, the party had gone off without a hitch and Wizzie had made so many new friends.

The women were sweet and generous, and already her social calendar was full for the rest of the month. Between lunches and teas and cookouts and brunches, why, if she only gained twenty pounds she'd be amazed!

She smiled, smoothing down the lines of her new red dress. She'd splurged on account of the home tour and even gotten new shoes to match. She knew Billy would be upset when the credit card bill came in, but it had been so long since she'd bought a pretty dress, and she'd gotten so many compliments on it, she was sure he wouldn't be too upset.

Women laughed as they began reaching for their coats and purses, all piled higgledy-piggledy on the downstairs guest room bed. Wizzie turned, smiled and winked at Billy as he and Booger finally snagged a finger sandwich from the snack table.

And then, from behind, a door slammed. Women screamed and gasped, clutching their pearls. Wizzie turned to find the guest bedroom door sealed tight. "Help them!" someone screamed, yanking on the doorknob to no avail. "They're trapped!"

"These old houses," Billy said, wading through the hysterical women, "you know how they can be when a draft blows through."

He smiled and Wizzie wanted desperately to believe him. And yet, tug as he might, face getting red even as Booger rushed to help, the door wouldn't budge.

"What should we do?" asked one of the members of the Southern Women's Hospitality League.

"Break it down?" offered another.

"Call 911!" said one more.

"Heavens no," said Amelia Honeycutt, hovering close to Wizzie and pinching the thick part of her arm. "I'm sure there's a simple explanation to—"

Just then the power went out, plunging the house into darkness save for the tiny tea candles flickering across the various coffee tables and snack bars that littered the living room floor.

The room erupted in screams as women stampeded for the front door, creating a hysterical logjam as Wizzie stood, mid-living room, watching Billy and Booger yank on the frozen guest room door.

Her heart pounded with the millions of things she should be doing—running, jumping, screaming, helping, soothing, calming— yet she couldn't move. The women toppled the snack tables trying to flee the house—her house—and yet she didn't once stop them and say, "Be careful, don't trip, proceed safely to the exits…"

Her head pounded with the incessant noise of the screaming and panicking, but it wasn't all human voices. As the crowd in the foyer finally managed to pry open the front door they were treated to a bright red glow Wizzie knew only too well.

"No," she murmured, drifting toward the door as the women bolted for their cars. "No, no, no…"

There, on the lawn, Chief Running Blood roared and chanted, dancing like a madman as the women scurried, leapt into their cars and spat gravel as they escaped with their very lives.

She slumped against the doorjamb, crying silently. Her heart was tight like someone was squeezing it, and she was sweaty, clammy, and breathing shallow. Behind her, Billy finally yanked the door open and out streamed more babbling women, screaming toward her. They passed her without a glance, trembling in fear at the giant Indian chief on the lawn as they raced to their cars.

The lawn spat beneath their tires, the smell of grinding gears and fresh sod rich in the air until the last guest was gone, her once successful home tour now a complete disaster.

Chief Running Blood turned to her, giant and red, a sneer across his face. "No more people on my land," he bellowed. "I tell you go, you stay. Not only stay, invite more white people to come."

"It's MY house," she shouted back, falling to her knees and pounding on the boards of the porch like a mad woman. "MY! HOUSE! You leave," she continued to scream, as Chief Running Blood stumbled back toward Wolf Creek. "YOU! LEAVE! NOW!"

Seeing him retreat in the face of her rage, she slumped, and the world grew dark and cold, so very, very cold.

Toni House

Chapter 50

Billy dropped to his knees at Wizzie's side, heart clenched in fear, and gripped her hand. It was clammy and moist, like a dishrag wrung mostly dry but not quite all the way.

"Wizzie," he said as Booger approached cautiously, face as pale and as drained of color as his stiff white dress shirt. "Honey, baby, come back to me."

He could feel her pulse, soft and weak, through her hand. He could see her breathing quietly as her eyes fluttered wildly beneath their lids.

"What should we do?" Booger asked, face drawn with concern.

"Let's get her into bed," Billy said, reaching for her hands.

"That's it?" Booger asked. "Shouldn't we call 911 or something?"

"She's a southern woman, Booger," Billy said, gritting his teeth as they hoisted her back into the house. "Southern women faint."

Booger grunted. "I heard that somewhere," he said as they carried her into the downstairs gust room.

It was a mess, what with all those women leaving behind half their jackets and purses. His stomach clenched, thinking of the hell there would be to pay tomorrow when they all came back looking for answers.

And poor Wizzie. She'd been so excited about the durn home tour, and here it had turned into some haunted house ride! Somehow Billy and Booger managed to slide the jackets and purses to one side and slip Wizzie under the covers.

There was a cane chair in the corner, some antique whatnot Wizzie had picked up their first year of marriage, and he pulled it next to her side before slumping heavily down into it.

"She looks a little better now," Booger whispered, hovering on the other side of the bed.

Billy smiled softly to himself, heart heavy. The kid was so earnest, so caring. He and Wizzie had talked often about having kids, but despite trying had never conceived. He wondered idly if Booger was the kind of kid they would have had: a little odd, a little weird, a lot caring.

"I don't think she slept more than three hours a night since she heard about the home tour," Billy said, nodding toward the distressed white rocking chair behind Booger.

He got the hint, moved aside some of Wizzie's famously homemade pillows, and slunk down inside. "Up before dawn every morning to shop and sew and clean and clean some more, then to bed late at night after planning on more sewing and shopping and cleaning before dawn the next day. She's just exhausted."

Billy heard the hopefulness in his voice, and so did Booger. "She's more than just exhausted," the kid said, avoiding Billy's eyes. "She's…she's probably in shock."

"Aren't we all?" Billy muttered, a cold, stone weariness settling in his bones. Then, in a rare moment of weakness, he looked across

Wizzie's sleeping body to catch Booger's eyes. "What are we going to do?" he asked, voice cracking.

Booger flinched at the sound, so uncommon and unexpected. "I don't know," he answered wearily, slumping down in the chair. "I thought…I thought we had protectors."

Billy's eyes grew heavy as he watched his wife breathe. "Some protectors," he murmured as his chin greeted his chest, his head too heavy to lift any longer. "Where are they when you need them?"

Chapter 51

Booger snapped to life, gripping the wooden rocking chair handles beneath his fingers. He sat up, hearing the steady breathing in the room. Candles still flickered from the party, illuminating Billy's sleeping face and Wizzie's weary smile.

He rose in the darkness, back sore from sleeping sitting up, and tried to see what time it was by the bedside clock. But it was digital and still blinking from the power outage during Chief Running Blood's tirade.

He glanced down at his watch and saw it was well after midnight. He groaned softly in the dark. If his mother was home, she was going to kill him!

Still, anxious as he was about missing curfew—again!—he leaned over Wizzie's peaceful frame and, with an index finger hovering above her lips, breathed a sigh of relief when warm air rushed across his skin.

Billy lay dead to the world, legs outstretched and slumped in the antique chair by Wizzie's bed. There was no need to feel for his breath; he snored like a lumberjack sawing logs.

Booger crept from the house, feeling bad about leaving it in such disarray with drinks spilled on the floor and cocktail napkins scattered everywhere, but he'd come back tomorrow and help clean up.

That was if he wasn't grounded for the rest of the year.

He avoided the front door, belly clenched in fear at the thought of facing Chief Running Blood again. Instead he slunk toward the sliding glass doors, most still half open as they'd been during the home tour.

Slipping through one, he crept down the patio steps and followed Wolf Creek toward his own house. The soft glow stopped him in his tracks a few yards away.

He gasped, so on edge from the events of the last few months he could hardly control his bodily functions at this point. There, one foot on the bank of Wolf Creek, stood Red Wolf.

"Stop," said the ghost, raising a faint hand. "Must talk."

"Talk is cheap," Booger huffed, though he stopped just the same. "Talk won't help my friends when Chief Running Blood is attacking them!"

Red Wolf paused, glowing under the pale moonlight, before bowing. "Power of Chief Running Blood still strong in death as it was in life," said the ghost brave, towering over Booger but somehow seeming smaller for a change.

Movement caught Booger's eyes and there, in the distance, just inside the tree line, lingered Tala, the giant wolf glowing red in the darkness.

Booger slumped against a tree, all the energy, all the bravery, wrung out of him. "So how can you protect us, then?" he asked meekly, looking at the ground.

"Need help," Red Wolf replied, standing tall. "Must help self."

"That's what we've been doing," Booger snapped, raising his eyes to meet Red Wolf's. "That's what we just did!"

Red Wolf didn't blink this time; he looked back, almost sadly. "Must find more help," he said, waving his hand for Booger to go. "Must find medicine man, cleanse this land, cleanse that house, set you free."

Booger felt momentarily hopeful, then instantly defeated. "Where do we find a medicine man?" he asked. "All the Indians are gone from here!"

Red Wolf shook his head sadly. "Not say you need live medicine man," he said, before shifting into mist. Seconds later his loyal ghost wolf followed, leaving Booger alone, cold and scared.

And in need of a dead medicine man.

Chapter 52

Booger cleared his throat. "You...you don't look like what I'd expect."

The man looked down at him, eyes kind and blue behind thick glasses. "You either," he said, welcoming him into his office. "You sounded older on the phone."

His name was Roger Eagle, and he was assistant professor of Native American Studies at Southern Regional University.

"You, too," said Booger, sitting in the seat across from the professor's messy desk.

The walls were covered with Native American art, framed photos of historic sites and vivid tapestries. Every bookshelf, filing cabinet and surface space was covered with old statues or pipes or bowls.

"You said you needed a medicine man?" Professor Eagle said, peering across his desk at Booger and wearing a curious expression.

Booger nodded, suddenly nervous. He was expecting someone old and senile, a withered man with long white hair and herbs in bags hanging from a medicine stick. Now he wasn't so sure.

"I-I live on land once hunted by the Mecklesh Clan," Booger began. "We…I think I'm being haunted by Chief Running Blood."

Professor Eagle's face grew a whiter shade of pale, and his chair creaked as he sat up slowly. "How do you know that name?"

"Same way I know yours," Booger said. "Google!"

"But I'm no medicine man," said Roger Eagle, nostrils flared, face still pale.

"But your father was," Booger said, rustling around in his backpack and sliding out some pages he'd printed in the school library. "And his father before him, and his father before him, dating back to the time when Chief Running Blood and the Mecklesh Clan ruled half of Alabama."

"My father's dead," Roger Eagle said, finally sitting back. "And as you can see, I'm a professor."

Booger slid forward on his seat, clinging to the printed pages. "But it's in your blood," he said. "I just…I need help, Mr. Eagle. I-I haven't slept in nights. Chief Running Blood's ghost haunts our land. I've seen him. My neighbors, Wizzie and Billy, have, too. Red Wolf says that we need a medicine man to cleanse the land so we can find peace and—"

"Red Wolf?" asked Roger Eagle, leaning forward until half his body was perched over his cluttered desk. "The history books say nothing of Red Wolf. I should know, I've written half of them." Haphazardly, almost absently, he pointed to a bookshelf full of hardbacks about the Mecklesh Clan. "How have you heard of him?"

"I haven't heard of him," Booger said. "I've *seen* him. Why? What's his story? Why wouldn't history know of him?"

"Because Chief Running Blood's legend was such that, even years after his death, none dared speak of his fiercest and only rival." Roger Eagle's eyes grew cloudy, and he peered above Booger's head. "Legend has it that Red Wolf had a pet—"

"A big wolf!" Booger said.

Roger Eagle focused on him for a moment, smirked, and shook his head. "Now how could you know that?"

"I've seen her, too."

Roger Eagle stared back skeptically then told his tale. "Stories say that Red Wolf had grown tired of doing Chief Running Blood's bidding. That his hatchet refused to scalp another innocent white man simply for living on, or sometimes even near, Mecklesh land. So he went to Chief Running Blood and pleaded with him, begged him, to make peace with the white folk, to share his land. Chief Running Blood grew enraged and attacked Red Wolf and even his sidekick, Tala. A bloody battle ensued until at last all three went over Dead Man's Cliff, never to be heard from again." His voice had grown soft and distant, as were his eyes.

"Until now," Booger said softly, too, to get the man's attention. "They're back, Mr. Eagle. All of them, or actually as Red Wolf told us, they never left."

The man shook his head, sitting back as if exhausted from his tale. "Impossible," he said, waving his hand. "That was hundreds of years ago."

Booger's heart was pounding. "Please," he begged voice scratchy and high. "Just spend one night on the banks of Wolf Creek with me. Just—"

"You live on Wolf Creek?" asked Roger Eagle, sitting up again.

"Yes," said Booger, heart ratcheting up another notch in his chest. "Why?"

"That's…" Roger Eagle stood up, reached for his coat and grabbed a book off a nearby stack. "That's where Chief Running Blood and Red Wolf fell after their battle at the edge of Dead Man's Cliff. That's…that's ground zero of Mecklesh Clan tribal folklore."

Roger Eagle stood at the door, one arm in his jacket, the book in his other hand, looking down at Booger still glued to his seat. "Aren't you coming?" he asked.

Booger had never moved so fast in his life.

Chapter 53

"Sorry," Booger said, dumping an armful of snack cakes and sodas at Roger Eagle's feet. "This is all I could find."

"What sorry?" the professor said, reaching down from his folding chair and grabbing a Choco-Berry Crunch. "I haven't had one of these in years."

Booger slid into the folding chair beside him and mumbled, "Well, I don't know, I mean, I wasn't sure what you ate."

Roger Eagle chuckled, chocolate and raspberry smeared across his teeth. "You mean what I eat as an assistant professor, as a grown man, or as a Native American?"

Booger blushed, glad the darkness of night covered it. "All the above, I guess."

"I eat what you eat, Booger," he said, folding his snack cake wrapper, and carefully slid it into the pocket of his jeans. "Just probably not as much."

Booger chuckled and tried not to creak in his chair. It was nearly midnight but the constant sodas and junk food he'd been eating since they arrived at Wolf Creek just after dark had him more wired than a hot rod on race day.

"Does your mother know you're out here?" Roger Eagle asked, looking behind them to Booger's darkened house.

"She does," Booger confessed. "Only she thinks I'm making a documentary about Native Americans for school. I hope you don't mind."

"Mind what?" Roger Eagle joked, reaching for another Choco-Berry Crunch. "That you used me in a lie without asking me? No, why would I?"

The professor had just grabbed the snack cake when the glow began beyond the trees. Booger tensed, wondering just whose glow it might be.

Meanwhile, Roger Eagle stood from his chair then slumped back down, dropping the snack cake to the ground. He stammered, face growing pale in the moonlight, as a giant wolf strode from the tree line, sniffing the ground before spotting Booger and the professor on the riverbank.

She stood, one paw slightly raised off the ground, glowing red nostrils flaring as beside her Red Wolf appeared, silent and stately as he regarded them both.

Roger Eagle was gasping, knuckles white as he gripped the arms of his chair. "I…" he croaked, looking from Booger back to Red Wolf and Tala, then back to Booger. "I…I can't believe it."

"Who dares speak in the presence of power?" asked Red Wolf.

"It is I," said the professor, standing at last to approach the ghost. "Son of Righteous Eagle, grandson of Warrior Eagle, great grandson of Wounded Eagle, descendant of his father, Hollow Eagle and his father before him, Mountain Eagle. I bow in the presence of the legend, Red Wolf, and his faithful companion, Tala."

Booger sat, mouth open. Roger Eagle's voice was firm and loud to match Red Wolf's. He bowed in deference, but not in fear. Red Wolf eyed him differently as well.

"I owe debt to Mountain Eagle," he said, bowing in return, his great red glow washing over the scrubby pines that littered the riverbank. "When Tala grew ill come sun season, great Mountain Eagle cured her when none others dared. If you are, as you say, from his blood, then I am honored to stand in your presence."

"It is I who is honored, Red Wolf, to be near the spirit of one who knew my kin."

Professor Eagle bent to one knee as Booger listened carefully.

"Who summons you?" Red Wolf asked.

Roger Eagle turned slightly, still kneeling, and nodded toward Booger. "It is the boy, oh powerful spirit. He wishes to cleanse this ground of the spirit of Chief Running Blood and sought my help."

"And now you seek mine?" asked Red Wolf, and Booger and Roger Eagle both nodded.

"Yes, oh powerful spirit. Help me honor the blood of my ancestors and cleanse this land once and for all."

"We search for your ancestor's herbal pot many years," Red Wolf said, voice soft and sad. "You must find. Use to cleanse land of Chief Running Blood's spirit. Only search when Tala visible. She will protect soul against evil one."

The professor nodded. "But how will I know when Tala is near?" he asked.

"She will find you, Roger Eagle," said Red Wolf, and the name sounded so regal and fine on his tongue it gave Booger the shivers. "Midnight hour beckons all spirits, good and bad."

With that, Red Wolf shimmered and, as quickly as he'd come, vanished into mist along the banks of Wolf Creek. Tala followed, turning mournfully and drifting behind him until their red glow was gone, leaving Roger Eagle kneeling in the moonlight.

Booger stood, waiting, until the professor joined him, hands trembling at his sides. "I'm sorry I doubted you," he said breathlessly, helping Booger fold the chairs back up and gather their snacks.

"When are you coming back?" Booger asked as they carried everything back to his house.

"Tomorrow," he said breathlessly. "And the next night, and the next, until I can find my ancestor's herbal pot and join my clan once more."

They stood awkwardly by Professor Eagle's car, a beat-up Jeep Wrangler from before Booger was born, probably. "Can I help?"

Roger Eagle chuckled, and opened his car door. "Only if you tell your mother the truth," he said.

Booger laughed. "Which is that I'm helping a tenth generation medicine man find an ancient herbal pot to banish three ghosts from our property?"

Roger Eagle nodded. "On second thought, let's stick with the documentary angle."

Booger smiled and watched his new friend drive away. Once he was gone and Booger was standing alone in the dark, his world felt very small and lonely. He wondered what Wizzie and Billy were up to, and if they would be happy that he had found the medicine man they were looking for.

Chapter 54

"How can I help you, Mr. Eagle?" Wizzie asked as she poured green tea into a ceramic mug on the patio. It was dusk, the sky over Wolf Creek bleeding orange into the water and red across the land.

Roger Eagle sat, regal and calm, in her favorite wicker chair. His skin was a burnished bronze, hair a sleek black peppered with gray and forming a long, intricate ponytail down the back of his faded denim shirt. He wore a tan vest over the shirt, two pockets on each side. When he smiled at her question, little laugh lines formed, thick and deep, around his rich brown eyes.

"Please, Mrs. Frank," he said, holding the tea gently in two hands. "Roger is fine. Mr. Eagle sounds so...*Dances With Wolves.*"

Wizzie snorted, then blushed, then covered her mouth with her hands. "But Roger just doesn't quite...fit," she said, admiring the turquoise clasp at his collar and the two leather straps that seemed to drip out of it and down the front of his shirt.

"Many call me 'Roger Eagle' as if it's one name," he offered.

"Then Roger Eagle it is," she said, pouring her own tea. "But only if you stop calling me Mrs. Frank and call me Wizzie instead."

"Certainly, Wizzie," he said and sipped his tea. He sighed with a satisfied sound and then reached for one of the fancy cookies she always kept on hand for unexpected guests. They were the same kind she served guests on Christmas Eve.

She reached for her favorite—shortbread dipped in dark chocolate and rolled in crushed almonds—and savored it before washing it down with her tea. She'd chosen green tea because it was the most natural thing she had in the house, but it went horribly with nice cookies.

"I should have served the Earl Grey instead," she said out loud before she could filter herself.

"What's that?" Roger Eagle asked.

"The tea," she confessed, blushing something awful. "I…I served the wrong tea."

"Let me guess," he said, reaching for another cookie, then two more. "You chose it because you figured a Native American would want something natural, right?"

She blushed and shook her head. "Does that make me an awful person?" she asked.

He chuckled, shaking his head. "No more awful than I am for drinking cherry soda at home."

She laughed and said, "I have some soda if you would like some?"

He waved her down as she slid toward the edge of her seat, about to get up. "Please, this is fine," he insisted, anxiously looking beyond the porch to the riverbank below. "I only came to introduce myself because Booger's told me so much about your…troubles."

Wizzie finished her cookie—she always liked to savor them— and washed it down with the bitter tea. "How much?" she asked.

Roger Eagle's face grew grim. "Pretty much everything," he admitted. "About Chief Running Blood, Red Wolf, Tala and…your sister." Their eyes met, hers suddenly moist, and he reached out a soft, papery hand to gently place it atop hers. "I'm very sorry for your loss, Wizzie."

Wizzie sat back in her chair, breathing heavily. "We've struggled for so long," she said, voice hoarse and tremulous, not the least bit shamed by her emotional reaction in front of a complete stranger. Loss will do that to a person, she'd always heard. Now she knew the truth firsthand.

"I hope I can help," he finally offered when Wizzie found herself at a loss for words, her sister Eve foremost in her mind's eye.

Wizzie sagged back in her chair, resting the teacup on the arm of her wicker chair. "I've almost given up hope," she said, voice deep and lost.

"I make no promises," Roger Eagle said gravely. "I wanted to come by and tell you that I have found a passage in one of the old journals passed down from my family that may have some answers, but I need to do a little more research in the morning when the Alabama Indian Affairs Commission's office opens."

Chapter 55

Roger Eagle turned on the private lane marked Deer Run Ridge and stopped in front of the Franks' home. He got out of his beat-up Jeep Wrangler, grabbed a large rolled-up paper tube and stuck it under his arm as he closed the door. "Hello all," he said as he walked up the front steps.

Billy stood and shook his hand. "Hi, Roger Eagle. I'm Billy. I really appreciate you taking the time to help us figure this out."

"Billy, like I told your wife last evening, I hope I can help but I cannot make any promises."

The professor sat in the chair next to Booger and across from Billy and Wizzie. "I have found a passage in one of the old journals that may tell us where my ancestor Warring Eagle's herbal pot rests." Reaching inside his vest pocket, he gently pulled out a stained and worn small leather journal that was tied around the center with a single leather strap and a weave of long black hair.

Roger Eagle paused, leafing through the ancient journal's wrinkled and yellow weathered pages. When he found the page he was looking for, he slipped bifocals out from another pocket, put them on the end of his nose, and read:

"... in the shadow of the light that hung in the night sky, on the first night of the full light in the night sky, must traverse a mighty muddy river where man and animal shared to drink together, two days' walk to meadow lands where man and beast lived and slept, to sacred grounds of mother earth, deer with eight horns, burial mound made with rocks and grass, medicine bag and herbal pot buried with the mighty medicine man, wrapped in a sacred hide next to his strong foot. If you dig under my bones, I will not be welcomed home to be born again."

He looked up, smiling, and removed his glasses.

"Is that…is that his diary?" asked Wizzie.

Roger Eagle smiled warmly before laughing. "No, no, Warring Eagle refused to record his thoughts, as did many of his sons. Only a few generations back, with my great, great, great grandfather, did the men of this family begin writing down the words of their forefathers."

Wizzie wrinkled her nose. "And where your ancestor left his herbal pot was worth noting?"

The professor nodded gravely. "This was no small matter," he said in a tone Wizzie could easily picture him using with his college students while giving a lecture on Native American culture. "A medicine man's herbal pot and medicine bag were sacred to him and to those he cured. It contained his very secrets and it would possess anything of spiritual value, like bones, arrowheads, an animal skin soaked in pure blood of the chief or of the medicine man, or maybe a pure-blood animal or even the hair of the chief or the hair of the medicine man himself. The only problem is that they always buried the herbal pot and the medicine bag with the medicine man."

Wizzie sat up a little straighter. "Wait, wait, what? We have to dig up this sacred herbal pot that is buried with this medicine man. We've lost our minds." She stood up quickly, put her hands on her hips, and then started pacing. "That's all we need is to disturb another *dead* Indian—no offense, Roger Eagle. Not only would we have this crazy chief trying to kill us, we would be *doomed* if we disturbed a medicine man's grave."

"Wizzie, normally you would be right", said Roger Eagle calmly. "But Warring Eagle knew that Chief Running Blood was just evil and one day he would have to be stopped. Of course, Warring Eagle had no idea it would be hundreds of years later, but he knew the secrets of how to cure—or kill—his chief would be needed."

"Why would Warring Eagle want to kill his chief?" Billy asked.

"He wouldn't," said Roger Eagle. "But if the chief did something to disgrace himself, or offend the tribal elders, or shame the tribe, it was Mecklesh custom for him to take the 'herb of sleep' and never wake up again."

"The herb of sleep?" Wizzie asked.

Roger Eagle looked down at his great, great, great grandfather's journal and nodded. "Venison root," he said, reading carefully. "Very rare these days, if not extinct, but quite common back in Warring Eagle's time."

Billy rubbed his temple. "This heavy scary stuff makes me want a beer. Would you like one, too, Roger Eagle?"

"Sure." He smiled.

"So," Billy said as he took a pull of his ice cold beer, "where do we find the grave of your ancestor?"

"I borrowed a map of the sacred burial grounds for the area around Wolf Creek and across to the other side of the Alabama River." He handed Booger the large paper tube and asked him to take the map out and lay it on the table. Then he handed Wizzie the journal. "Turn to the page where the feather is sticking out," he instructed. "Now read the passage again. And, Billy, I need you to follow the instructions on the map."

Wizzie read:

"'... *in the shadow of the light that hung in the night sky, on the first night of the full light in the night sky, must traverse a mighty muddy river where man and animal shared to drink together, two days' walk to meadow lands where man and beast lived and slept, to sacred grounds of mother earth, deer with eight horns, burial mound made with rocks and grass, medicine bag and herbal pot buried with the mighty medicine man, wrapped in a sacred hide next to his strong foot. If you dig under my bones, I will not be welcomed home to be born again.*'"

"Okay, wait," Booger said, "'... *in the shadow of the light that hung in the night sky.*'" Booger rubbed his head. "What's the shadow?"

"I actually think it means in the shadow of the moon," Roger Eagle said.

"'...*on the first night of the full light in the night sky, must traverse a mighty muddy river...*'" Wizzie furrowed her brow trying to piece together each clue. "The first night of the full moon?" she asked.

"I think so," said Roger Eagle, "and we have to cross a mighty river. I'm assuming the Alabama River. '...*two days' walk to meadow lands*'—that's two days' walk to the valley—'...*to sacred grounds, deer with eight horns'*—sacred burial grounds marked with something that looks like a deer with eight horns."

"What's a burial mound made with rocks and grass?" Wizzie asked.

"Many native tribes buried their important people in burial mounds. A burial mound is a room-like structure that has been dug into the side of a mountain, or in the earth, that is also built with rocks, mud and grass and can have as many as ten or eleven people buried in one," Roger Eagle explained.

"*'Medicine bag and herbal pot buried with the mighty medicine man'*—this one is self-explanatory," he continued. "'*...wrapped in sacred hide next to his strong foot...*' I believe this means his right foot, at least I hope he was right-handed. '*If you dig under my bones, I will not be welcomed home to be born again.*' This one is also self-explanatory."

Booger took out a notebook from his backpack and wrote all the clues in the order they were read.

...in the shadow of the moon...

...the first night of the full moon...

...cross the Alabama River...

...two days' walk to the valley...

...to sacred burial grounds, marked by a deer with eight horns...

...a burial mound made with rocks and grass...

...Medicine bag and herbal pot buried with the mighty medicine man, in a sacred hide next to his right foot...

...must not dig under medicine man's bones...

Roger Eagle read them. "I think we need to move some around in a different order, like we need to cross the river first, then we need to walk two days to the valley in the shadow of the moon—I believe that means in the shadow of the full moon—we locate the deer with eight horns, and then the first night after the full moon we should be able to see the burial mound. Hopefully the herbal pot is buried separately next to his right foot."

"No, no this is wrong, and besides we could go to jail for disturbing scared burial grounds. No, there has to be another way," Wizzie said. "We cannot do this."

"Wizzie, we have no choice." Billy's voice was soft and low. He placed his hand on her shoulder.

She looked up at him. "Billy, this is wrong."

"I know," he whispered again, "but we have no choice."

"We will meet here tomorrow night. We can take my Jeep as far as possible before we have to walk." Roger Eagle put the journal back in his vest and picked up the map. "Until tomorrow night." He waved.

Chapter 56

There came a rustle at the steps of the porch and Wizzie smiled to see Booger, backpack in hand, looking similarly geared up for his several nights' work.

"Hi, Wizzie," he said with a bashful grin as he climbed the porch steps one by one. "You ready, Roger Eagle?"

"Are you?" the professor joked. "And by the way, what story did you tell your mom this time?"

"Hmm, well, I told her that I am working with you on a documentary for one of your books and you were going to see if you could get me extra credit in history class."

"That's doable. I'm sure I could talk with your history teacher and get you those extra credit points. But does she know that all of us are going? And that you will be gone for at least three days?"

"She does," replied Billy. "I spoke with her this morning. I told her we needed his assistance with locating the herbal pot."

"You told her the truth?" asked Booger.

"Of course I did, Booger. Your mom knows what's going on. She's okay as long as you are with the three of us and you are not in any danger. We are just looking for a herbal pot—it's a camping and hiking trip," Billy explained.

"Are we all ready?" Roger Eagle stood and grabbed his own backpack from where it had been sitting next to his chair.

"Sure thing," Booger said, as if it was a normal camping trip and not one where they had to decipher ancient clues to help them search for an ancient herbal pot buried by one of Roger Eagle's ancestors. "Flashlights, canteen, snack cakes, more snack cakes, sleeping bags, sandwiches, two small ice chests and toiletries. Do we need anything else?"

Wizzie looked puzzled. "I'm confused," she said. "I thought we had to wait for Tala to appear before you could search."

Roger Eagle and Booger looked at her as if she were speaking Ancient Mecklesh. Then they both sagged into deck chairs to wait.

Chapter 57

Wizzie had just finished brewing a second pot of coffee when she returned to the porch. Roger Eagle was slumped over, sleeping quietly, while Booger held out his cup silently.

"You've had enough," Wizzie whispered, wondering what his poor mother must think of the "crazy neighbor lady" who spent so much time with her kid. "You should be sleeping, like them." She nodded toward Roger Eagle and Billy.

"I can't sleep now," Booger hissed as she filled his cup, but only halfway. "This stuff is great!"

He slurped it noisily and finished another of the gooey chocolate snack cake he'd brought along for the treasure hunt. The kid would be lucky if he ever went back to sleep.

She sat down and sipped her own coffee, feeling somehow safe and protected with Roger Eagle, and Billy and even Booger nearby. It was nearly 2 a.m. and still no Tala. She couldn't control what happened in her world anymore, but she could control who she let inside it and the more friends and family she could have around, the better.

She was reaching for one of Booger's snack cakes—if you can't beat 'em, join 'em—when his glasses reflected an eerie red glow.

"Booger?" she said, voice high, hand still clasping the uneaten coconut cream pie. "I think…I think…"

"Tala," said Roger Eagle, voice tense as he rose from his seat. He seemed to have awakened with the ghostly wolf's giant red presence. "She's here. Our hunt can begin."

They all piled in the professor's Jeep and followed the wolf as she crossed over to the other side of the river. Tala stood and waited. Traveling by Jeep the foursome had to go the long way around and cross the bridge over the Alabama River. Roger Eagle pulled the Jeep onto an old, very narrow, rocky dirt road, and they could see Tala's red glow off in the distance as she stood and waited for them. He drove as far and long as he could until the small rocky road no longer existed. It dead-ended into the mountain face.

"Okay," he said, "everybody out and grab a camping pack."

The three men had larger packs and Billy helped Wizzie slip the smaller one on her back.

"Wizzie!" hissed Booger. "It's not safe."

"Our protector is here," she insisted, reaching for one of the jangling flashlights clinking in his pack. "I'm as safe as you are."

"She's right," said Roger Eagle, holding a flashlight as well. "Only the Great Spirits can protect us now."

The flashlights proved pointless as Tala's vibrant red glow illuminated the entire mountain ridge. "Where's Red Wolf?" asked Booger as they crept along the edge of the mountain trail.

"Perhaps he's somewhere else," Wizzie suggested. "Protecting us from Chief Running Blood?"

"But he and Tala are always together," Booger pointed out, making Wizzie nod then pause for thought.

"Booger, you are right. It's unusual for Red Wolf not to be with Tala, or maybe the chief just wants us to stay off the land that's close to the house."

"We don't need to see the Great Spirits to sense their presence," Roger Eagle said confidently. "We must only trust their guidance and receive the gift of their protection."

Booger and Wizzie shared a glance behind Roger Eagle's back. They had seen Chief Running Blood's destruction firsthand; he hadn't. And still they walked, carefully, slowly, along the side of the mountain as they continued to climb.

Tala sniffed and breathed and wheezed, trailing tendrils of cold, thin mist as her paws crept along the mountain, leaving no prints behind. Not for the first time, Wizzie shook her head in disbelief.

Here she was, at two in the morning, crouching between a ninth grader and a Native American Studies professor, and Billy up ahead of her, looking for an ancient medicine man's herbal pot while being guided by a giant, glowing red wolf ghost!

They were far from the Franks' house now, and even farther from Booger's, as they continued to climb up toward the top of the mountain. Wizzie asked the group to stop so she could pull out the map and look at the clues.

"Okay," she said, "it appears we are going the right way. We have to climb to the top of this mountain ridge and back down the other side to the valley below."

"No, Wizzie, there is a small trail about halfway up the mountain that crosses over to the other side." Roger Eagle traced the line with his finger.

"Good," she said. "We wouldn't make it to the meadowlands by tomorrow night without the shortcut."

"Wizzie, we won't be there by tomorrow night." Billy smiled. "It should take two days to walk to the meadowlands, but right here"—he pointed on the map—"are cabins that we can sleep in. We need to get to the meadowlands or the valley before it gets black dark on the third day. We need to be in position so when the shadow of the full moon falls over the valley we can find the deer with eight horns. If we miss it, it will be another month before we can try again. I am reading this right, aren't I, Roger Eagle?"

"Right you are, Billy. At least, that is the way I am deciphering the passage in the journal."

Tala paused, giant ghostly red tail wagging as she sniffed wildly in the air. She waited patiently for the foursome to get moving again then she leapt forward and upward. Wizzie and the rest of her search party followed.

Chapter 58

"There's the valley," Roger Eagle said, winded, as he pointed toward the lush green land.

Wizzie sat on the flat part of a large slanted boulder that overlooked the valley. The grass blew like waves in the wind, the valley floor covered with white and yellow and pink and purple wild flowers, as if an artist had painted a portrait. The colors were breathtakingly beautiful. It was still warm even when the foursome sat under a complete canopy of trees that covered the mountain trail.

Amid a symphony of birds singing, wild rabbits scurrying and ground squirrels foraging for nuts, Tala stopped a short distance away, far enough to keep from freezing Wizzie but still protectively close. Wizzie lay back on the boulder and closed her eyes. It was the most relaxed and peaceful she had felt for months. The rhythm of nature's symphony and the breeze lulled her to sleep.

Billy heard Wizzie's small deep breath and a slight snore, and he smiled. He put his finger over his mouth to let Roger Eagle and Booger know to be quiet. Billy took a long-sleeve shirt from his pack and covered Wizzie's shoulders. It was long enough that it reached a little past her waist.

Roger Eagle pulled out the map and leather journal and spread them out on the dirt ground. He held the map in place with a rock on each corner to keep the wind from blowing it away like a wayward kite.

"Billy, you need to stand here, on the valley floor." He pointed at a place on the map. "Booger, you need to stand on the mountain here." He pointed at another spot on the map and indicated Booger should stand a few feet up the rise. "Wizzie will need to stay here, where we are. And I will walk to the valley floor on this side. That way we can cover the whole mountainside and the meadow. Wizzie and Booger should be able to see the whole valley with them being at a higher elevation. It's important that we find the deer with eight horns.

"Billy, it's time to wake Wizzie and for each of us to take up our stations." Roger Eagle reached in his camp pack and handed them each a pair of binoculars, a flashlight, a whistle and a walkie-talkie.

Billy chuckled, turned his walkie-talkie on, and helped Booger with his. "I haven't seen these in a few years. Nowadays everybody uses cell phones."

Chapter 59

The night grew still and quiet, and Wizzie heard her own heartbeat thumping in her ears. She stood and tapped her foot as she twisted the whistle that hung from her neck. Eyes wide, she turned her head back and forth as she watched for the moon to rise, and swatted at a mosquito buzzing near her face. The katydids and crickets sang their evening songs and Tala stood at a protective distance. As the moon rose, Wizzie covered her mouth with her hand and basked in its magnificent glory. The moon was a brilliant orange-red with gray shadows that appeared to make a sleepy face.

It was a perfect round sphere with the bottom quarter hidden by the lush green valley. The earth appeared to come to a dead end and you could walk off its edge and straight into the moon. The enormous mass encompassed the entire side of the earth and appeared to be too large for the sky.

"There!" Wizzie screeched. She pointed toward Billy and Booger, then snatched the walkie-talkie from her pocket and pushed the button. "Billy," she shouted into the walkie-talkie. "The deer, the deer is above your head to the right. Booger is standing on top of the head."

The light from the moon was just right to catch the whitish glare that reflected back at her. She peered through her night binoculars and the tips of some whitish-gray horns appeared. As the moon continued to rise, she could see what looked to be an elongated body with darker wavy shadows that moved as if the deer was breathing. She could also see a smaller rock with an oval-shaped black smudge that appeared to blink as it stared back at her. Wizzie gasped.

Chapter 60

Tala ran ahead of her as she ran down the mountain to the valley below. "Tala, wait," Wizzie yelled. "I can't run as fast as you. I don't float. I have to crawl over or around the rocks and boulders, and I'm not a ghost—I can't go through them either."

Tala turned and looked at Wizzie and gave her long tail a quick flick as if to tell Wizzie to stop complaining and hurry.

As she got closer to the rock formation, the deer seemed to disappear. "Booger," Wizzie yelled, out of breath, into the walkie-talkie. "Don't move. The head was under your left foot."

Billy pointed the flashlight beam under Booger's feet but nothing but the side of the mountain appeared in front of him. He rubbed the rock with his hand. It wasn't horns but petrified tree branches bleached out from long days and years in the sun. They were hundreds or thousands of years old, and the base of the tree branches looked to adorn a crown as though it perched on top of a skull. Each branch snaked out like a spiderweb that led to exactly eight points.

Billy stood back from the rock formation and it disappeared again. "Wow," he said. "You know the formation is there but you can't see it. Unless you were looking for it, you would never notice it."

"You're right, Billy," said Roger Eagle. "I suspect that's the reason my ancestors chose the deer with eight horns to be seen only by moonlight, because they never wanted the burial mound found."

"Of course your ancestors didn't," said Wizzie, "but that's exactly what we're doing."

Chapter 61

Billy pulled a small blanket out of his camping pack and laid it on the ground for Wizzie to sit on. "Here, Baby Dolly," he whispered. He had never seen her in such disarray: clothes wrinkled and dirty, no makeup on, and her straight blond hair was sweat-soaked and flat against her head. Wizzie never thought of him as a horrible husband and he took pride in providing and protecting her. But today he wasn't so sure anymore.

"Do we need to stand in the same places tonight as last night?" Booger asked.

"I don't believe so. We should be able to see the burial mound from where the deer with eight horns is located," Roger Eagle said. "But I need you to stand on the mountain ten feet higher."

The foursome stood at the far end of the meadow as the moon rose, the birds stopped their evening song and crickets strummed an energetic march. The moon again encompassed the entire side of the earth as it had done the night before. It made the four people appear minuscule in its enormous size like a tiny cork bobbing in the ocean. It made Wizzie want to reach out and touch it.

"There!" Booger shouted and pointed to the far end of the meadow toward a thick row of huge trees. "Look between the trees."

They looked in the direction where Booger had pointed.

"The burial mound is over there," Booger shouted again.

The cloudy night sky obscured the reflective light. As the moon continued to rise higher and higher, the yellow glow faded into a muted white light. Booger made his way to the meadow and ran to the large trees.

"The burial mound is here," he shouted over his shoulder toward the other three.

"Are you sure, Booger? We never saw it," Billy said.

"I'm sure." Booger dropped to his knees and put his face in his hands.

"Young man, if you say you saw it, then it's here somewhere," Billy assured him. "Have you ever seen oak trees so big in your life?" Billy's comment was more a statement than a question.

Then the clouds moved enough to allow the moon's light to shine in between the trees. The reflection of a hidden mound of rocks blinked on then went off again.

"There!" Wizzie pointed.

"I saw it, too," Roger Eagle and Billy said at the same time.

Chapter 62

Booger grunted then cursed.

"Booger!" Wizzie hissed maternally, though he wasn't her child. "Language!"

"But I found it," he said, digging furiously as Wizzie abandoned her own spade and hustled over. "I found the herbal pot," he insisted, then said more doubtfully, "I think…"

Wizzie looked down as Roger Eagle joined them. It was still dark and the three of them shone their flashlights into the shallow hole Booger had been digging. There was a stiff piece of leather hide, part creamy beige and part a rusty black color like dried tar. The pot was clay, a kind of rust color against the rich, dark earth in which it had lain for decades. On it were dozens of symbols, some unknown to her but others looking like crude portraits of running deer and crouching bears.

Booger's flashlight beam wavered then danced as he looked up at Roger Eagle apologetically. "I think I broke it."

Wizzie had to admit that a strange, funky smell was coming from a small crack in the top of the pot.

"Anything could have done that," Roger Eagle said quietly as he reached into the ground to retrieve the pot.

"Aren't you going to use gloves or anything?" Booger asked.

The professor chuckled. "Booger, you watch too many movies."

Still, his hands were trembling slightly as he lifted the herb pot from the ground and laid it on the grass. Behind them, red light glowed as Tala slowly approached.

Roger Eagle gently pried open the top and a hiss of dust and stale air escaped. Wizzie held her nose and Booger retched, but Roger Eagle and Billy bent eagerly to inspect the contents of the pot.

"Not much here," he said, disappointedly. "Time has turned the herbs to dust. I can't tell one from the other."

Billy took time to put everything back in the burial mound, trying to make it appear that no one had disturbed the sacred ground.

"What does that mean?" asked Booger.

Roger Eagle shrugged. "I don't know, really. I…this is all a little beyond my job description."

Wizzie nodded. She should have known not to expect too much from Roger Eagle, or anyone else for that matter. Chief Running Blood was too strong, too powerful, for anyone to help them.

"But," the professor said, and Wizzie's heart lifted with hope, "Red Wolf said to find the herbal pot, and we've found the pot."

"Now we just have to figure out what to do with it," Booger said.

"You must bring back to burial site of Chief Running Blood," said a voice behind them. Wizzie leapt, brushing against Booger as they both turned to see Red Wolf standing next to his beloved Tala.

The two ghosts glowed a violent red, their features more distinct in the dead of night. Roger Eagle bowed instinctively before kneeling before the two spirits. Wizzie, Booger and Billy exchanged a glance before bowing then kneeling as well.

"And then what, great spirit warrior?" asked Roger Eagle, his tone serious and grave.

"Find the words to the ancient cleansing ritual and chant them around the herbal pot."

He nodded, even as Wizzie's heart beat harder. Her head bent low, she only knew that the ghosts had gone by the absence of red light all around them.

Still, long after the spirit warriors had gone, the foursome remained silent.

"What does that mean, Roger Eagle?" Wizzie asked, voice sounding too desperate for her taste.

He stood and helped her up. "It means I have to go back to my ancestor Warring Eagle's journal." He sighed. "And find the words to the cleansing ritual."

Booger and Wizzie frowned. "Can we help?" Booger asked, gathering up the shovels into his backpack and hoisting it over his shoulder.

"We will meet in a few nights at the top of Dead Man's Cliff," Roger Eagle said. "It will take us at least three days to get back home."

"Will you find it by then?" Booger asked, trying to keep up.

"Warring Eagle only kept a few slim journals," he said, his flashlight beam stretching only a few inches in front of his feet. "So if I can't find it there, I'm not sure where else to look."

Chapter 63

Roger Eagle felt excited several nights later when he arrived, leather journal in hand, for their nightly vigil.

"Roger Eagle," Wizzie said as Billy rose, extending a hand. "Did you find something?"

"I'm glad you're all here because tonight we're going to need all the help we can get."

"Why's that?" asked Booger as he slid through the screen door with a fresh can of soda in his hand. Wizzie shot him a withering look, but he opened it anyway.

"I found the cleansing ritual in Warring Eagle's journals." Roger Eagle beamed, waving the green, leather-bound journal in his hand. "But it says the more voices chanting it, the more powerful it becomes."

"Will four of us be enough?" Wizzie asked anxiously, rising to join her husband.

"It will have to be," the professor said wearily. "I don't know how many more of these late nights I can take."

"You and me both," said Billy, who'd just gotten home from his new job as chief of security. He looked handsome in his charcoal gray jeans and light blue shirt, but weary.

"I also found something new," Roger Eagle said quieter, so that Wizzie and Booger had to inch forward to hear him. "Something that might explain what started the feud between Chief Running Blood and Red Wolf."

Wizzie felt nervous. She had known Red Wolf and the great, bloody chief as ghosts, spirits, specters that haunted her dreams— both while asleep and awake. To think that they had shared the same earth, sat around the same fire, gave her the chills.

"What is it?" asked Booger, excited, leaning on the porch rails.

Roger Eagle opened the slim leather volume and turned the thick, yellowed pages that sounded stiff. He found a page midway through the journal. "Chief Running Blood had a daughter named Winter Snow, because of the single strand of white hair she was born with. Winter Snow was promised to wed the warring Checklan tribe's fittest brave, Hawk Feather, in a pact to seal longstanding tensions between both tribes. But little did Chief Running Blood know that Red Wolf and Winter Snow had fallen in love. When he found out, Chief Running Blood was furious. He lured Red Wolf to the top of Dead Man's Cliff where they fought to their death."

"No wonder they stick around haunting the place," said Booger with awe in his voice. "They must still be so angry at each other."

"But why didn't Winter Snow stop her father?" Wizzie asked.

"Or haunt him?" asked Billy. "Like the others?"

Roger Eagle shook his head, flipping forward in the leather journal. "After Chief Running Blood's death, Winter Snow kept his wishes and married Hawk Feather."

"Oh." Wizzie gasped, shaking her head. "What a tragic ending."

"For her, perhaps," said Roger Eagle. "But her marriage ended the friction between both tribes, which ultimately led to reconciliation with white settlers. Modern Wilcox County owes a debt to the sacrifice Winter Snow made to make peace among the land."

"Hard to believe she was Chief Running Blood's daughter," Booger said, shaking his head.

"That still doesn't explain why she didn't haunt this land," Billy said, frowning.

"She must have died a peaceful death," Booger explained. "Which would leave her no reason to stick around, right?"

"Who says she doesn't?" Wizzie huffed.

Booger looked from adult face to adult face, searching for answers, but Wizzie had none.

"You're the ghost expert," she said. "You tell us."

"It doesn't matter now," said Roger Eagle, finding the page he had marked. "We must take the herbal pot and stand around it, chanting the cleansing ritual."

Wizzie nodded, looking to Billy. He nodded, and then so did Booger.

Still, Roger Eagle didn't budge. "I must warn you," he said, looking from one to the other before speaking again. "The cleansing ritual is a fierce and powerful spell and works almost instantly. I...I would try to do it myself if I thought it would work with one voice."

Wizzie nodded. "But a lone voice isn't a chant, is it, Roger Eagle?"

"No, Wizzie, it's not."

"Then let's go," said Billy, hitching up his new work pants and taking Wizzie's hand. "Stick by me, honey britches, and let's get this durn mess over with once and for all."

They walked quietly until they found a clearing just past Wizzie's and Billy's house at the foot of Dead Man's Cliff.

"Here," said Roger Eagle, asking Wizzie to place the herbal pot on the ground.

"Ouch," Wizzie murmured. She pulled a large sliver of clay from her hand, leaving a partial bloody handprint on the side of the pot.

Roger Eagle extended his hands on either side. "Form a circle," he instructed, almost stern, "and hold hands."

When they were standing in a circle, holding hands, Booger asked, "What about the ritual?"

Roger Eagle smiled. "I memorized it," he said, winking at the boy. And then, as if clearing his face, his expression went blank. They stood in silence, listening to a slight breeze rustle through the oak leaves high above on Dead Man's Cliff until Roger Eagle began. "Oh mystic mountains, high above, send us your strength. Oh powerful spirits, all around, give us permission to cleanse this land free of evil, now and forever—"

Gradually the wind increased, whipping Wizzie's hair in her face and forcing her to clutch onto Billy and Booger's hands to keep from flying away.

Roger Eagle kept right on going, speaking louder as he finished. "Cleanse this land free of evil, now and forever, and return it to its rightful owners." He looked at them again, his long hair blowing in the breeze. "Repeat after me," he said, starting the chant over. "Oh mystic mountains, high above, send us your strength..."

They spoke the chant, word by word, line by line, voice by voice. "Oh powerful spirits, all around, give us permission to cleanse this land..."

With each voice and each word, the wind blew harder until the trees bent, until they couldn't stand, until at last the herbal pot fell over, spilling its ancient dust into the wind.

But it didn't disperse. Instead, it grew and multiplied into a fine mist.

"Don't stop!" Roger Eagle shouted above the rising wind as they paused in their chanting to admire the growing green mist. "Keep chanting!"

"Oh mystic mountains, high above, send us your strength…" They continued until the mist grew and spread and seemed to cover the land.

"It's working!" Booger shouted. "It's working. Look!"

"Booger! Keep! Chanting!"

They chanted, and the mist covered the grass at their feet, cold and slimy as it slid along their ankles and shoes. And still they chanted, until a faint red glow began to shine and Wizzie felt the hairs on the back of her neck stand on end.

"Stop this at once!" bellowed Chief Running Blood. Wizzie felt Booger's hand tear from her own as he screamed, turning away from the giant, glowing ghost.

Roger Eagle stood frozen, mouth half open in mid-chant. Wizzie continued to recite the cleansing ritual, murmuring under her breath as Billy pushed her behind him. "Oh mystic mountains, high above, send us your strength…"

Chief Running Blood growled and glowed, fearsome in his giant headdress and muscular torso, standing at the water's edge. Wizzie watched as Roger Eagle stood, not bowing in the face of his ancestor's former chief.

"Oh Great Chief Running Blood," he began, voice strong and firm. "Chief of the Mecklesh tribe, leave this land once and for all."

Chief Running Blood raged and swung his battle axe. Wizzie screamed and Billy leapt and Roger Eagle ducked, but the glowing red axe sliced at his arm and knocked him to the ground.

Billy stood over him, arms up as if to box, and Wizzie chanted mercilessly, whispering the entire while. Chief Running Blood laughed, raising his axe again, until another red glow filled the riverbank and a growl echoed through the night.

Axe high overhead, the chief glanced up just in time to see Tala launching her ghostly self through the air like fiery red electric flames. She snarled and bit into the chief's arm, but the giant warrior tossed the massive wolf aside and pounced until they rolled on the ground, stirring up dirt and the green mist that seemed to cover the entire property.

The ghosts battled, blurry and fierce and bloody and real and not real. Between clenched eyes and muttering lips, Wizzie chanted while Booger and Billy helped Roger Eagle to his feet.

"The pot," he said weakly, face pale and blood dripping from the gash in his arm. "Throw it at the chief! It will banish him."

"We can't!" Booger said, watching the fierce ghosts battle in the dirt. "What about Tala?"

Just then Red Wolf appeared on the bank, war paint on his face, flowing black locks around his bare shoulders. "Tala!" he hissed and, yelping, the giant beast leapt from the green and red mist to join his master at his side.

"Now!" Roger Eagle said and Booger tossed the ancient herbal pot at Chief Running Blood.

It sailed through the air, mist trailing and surrounding it. As Chief Running Blood stood, vengeance in his eyes, he saw the pot and bellowed. His eyes were wide and he screamed as it sailed right into his chest.

There was a gasp and a roar, an explosion of light and the smell of burnt flesh. And still Wizzie chanted, fists clenched so tight she dug white crescent moons into the palms of her hands. The glow was so bright she shut her eyes and turned, still chanting, as a burst of light and heat and ash filled the air.

Then a loud burst of red electric flames lit up the black sky, the wind blew at a gale force, and Chief Running Blood was standing and staring down at them, laughing the most sinister laugh. It was so evil and so loud Wizzie covered her ears.

"You will never get rid of me," Chief Running Blood bellowed. "You can never defeat me, Wizzie Frank, and you will die when I am ready for you to die."

Wizzie had fallen on her knees, sobbing and trembling. "Why are you doing this?" Her voice carried away with the wind.

"All white people will die. I will kill them all, like I did the white woman. I warned you."

Tears streamed down Wizzie's cheeks, leaving black smoke streaks down her face as she crawled on the ground. She found and picked up the old journal tied with a leather strap and a weave of long black hair. She crawled over to where the fire was and picked up the fire starter, then ripped the leather strap and weave of black hair off the journal and clicked the fire starter.

"What are you doing?" roared Chief Running Blood.

She clicked the fire starter again and this time she held it to the long black hair. The hair caught fire. It singed and smoked and shriveled up, and thick red and gray smoke filled the sky as she threw the leather strap and hair to the ground.

Chief Running Blood screamed, "No—no—no!"

As the hair burned more, the chief's body burned and his flesh melted. The smell of charred flesh and death filled the air. His body turned into ash, and the flames licked at the night sky.

Wizzie turned and blinked, but by then it was over. The sky was dark, the chief gone, and with him Tala and Red Wolf.

Chapter 64

It was a quiet affair, simple and sweet. The house was aglow with flickering candles and soft music but inevitably they all found their way onto the porch.

More candles flickered and screen doors let the soft jazz from inside ooze out while Wizzie's carefully prepared platters of sausage and cheese, crackers and fruit slowly disappeared.

Billy drank his beer, slow and cold, from a cooler at his feet. He'd taken the weekend off, a rare perk after working almost a year at the plant. He looked soft and relaxed in a new checkered shirt and old jeans, his hair cut short and his face tan from working in the yard all day.

Roger Eagle sat next to him, spiffy as always in khaki slacks and a crisp white shirt, a turquoise necklace just visible beneath his open collar. His hair was pulled back into a severe ponytail, leaving his lined face exposed and almost fragile. He drank a glass of wine slowly, while nibbling on some aged Gouda from the bread plate on the wicker table next to him.

Booger sat quietly as well, peering past the porch railing to the gently lapping waters of Wolf Creek, dark now, illuminated only by a half-full moon and, perhaps, the flickering torches at the end of the stairs.

Wizzie wanted plenty of light every night. In the weeks since they had banished Chief Running Blood from their property, and apparently Red Wolf and Tala as well, she had gotten a little stronger and then a little stronger still.

But she still feared the darkness that fell each night, and insisted that Billy fill her nights with light. So more candles than ever lined the porch, and he'd put little torch pots along the railing, filled with kerosene and flickering every few feet.

She gazed at them now, a smooth saxophone solo sounding quietly at her back, the lapping water at her front, surrounded by friends and family.

On his favorite porch step, Budweiser snuffled and snapped at a lazy dragonfly that had come to rest on the chocolate lab's snout. The insect buzzed away but the dog was too lazy to pursue it, which left a smile on Wizzie's face.

"All this time later," she said, the first one to speak in minutes, "and we all still seem so tuckered out."

Roger Eagle laughed gently, putting his glass down on the table next to his cheese plate. "I find my mind wandering in class," he confessed with a shy smile. "I want to tell my students what happened, even though I know none of them will believe me."

Billy chuckled, nodding from his own deck chair. "Try wandering around a lonely plastics factory," he said, before finishing his beer. "I keep expecting a rosy glow to appear around every corner, or a wolf to howl while I'm fixing myself a cup of coffee in the break room."

"Try being home alone all day." Wizzie huffed a little more harshly than she'd intended. "Seeing shadows in every room, waiting for the sliding glass doors to blow in!"

"I thought I saw a red glow the other morning," Booger confessed, turning toward them as he wiped cookie crumbs off his blue lined track pants. "But it was just a cop car pulling someone over down the street."

They all nodded silently, lost in thought. "I guess we're all still a little spooked," Billy said, reaching for Wizzie's hand. She took it gratefully and they lingered there, clinging to one another's strength.

"Do you...can it really be over?" Wizzie asked hopefully, speaking for the group.

One by one, they turned to Roger Eagle. He held his hands up defensively and said, "I'm not the expert here, remember? But, honestly, we did everything the old books said, and it didn't work. However, Wizzie, if you wouldn't mind answering some questions, how did you know to burn the weave of hair?"

"I didn't," Wizzie replied. "I cut my hand on the herbal pot and some of my blood was on it when we threw it at Chief Running Blood's chest, but it only made him stronger. I was so scared; all I wanted to do was crawl into a ball and hide. When I fell to the ground I found the journal and then your story of the sacred pot, blood and hair flashed in my head so I yanked the weave of hair from the journal, rubbed some of my blood on it, and lit it on fire."

"Whose hair was in the weave?" Booger asked.

"Probably both the chief's and the medicine man's. I also think that the animal hide may have been soaked in pure blood, but from whom I don't know, and with Wizzie's blood something worked. Wizzie, you have earned an A-plus for listening in class." Roger

Eagle chuckled, which caused them all to laugh nervously. "But is it over? Who knows?"

They all nodded, but Wizzie's stomach still felt clenched. Although she slept better and longer at night, there was often a tight feeling in the pit of her stomach. Every night she counted her blessings that they'd survived another day, and yet she woke up every morning convinced they wouldn't survive the next.

She kept waiting for the other shoe to drop, and it seemed she wasn't alone.

"But what if they come back?" Billy asked, squeezing Wizzie's hand. "I just can't help feeling it isn't over yet."

Roger Eagle nodded, posture slightly stooped as if he hadn't been sleeping well either. "The spirit world is vast and unknown," he admitted, rubbing his eyes. "Perhaps they will always be there, lurking in the shadows. Perhaps we banished them to another realm for good. Only time will tell."

Wizzie almost groaned; it was far from the declarative statement she wanted to hear.

"But what about Red Wolf?" Booger persisted. "And Tala? Why did the good ghosts have to go?"

The professor shrugged. "Perhaps they followed Chief Running Blood to keep him away from us. Maybe they're protecting us right now."

As if on cue, the brush along the riverbank rustled. Wizzie sat up on high alert and clung tightly to Billy's hand. Budweiser barked and, in so doing, roused a raccoon from the tree line. The dog growled and leapt as the furry creature lit out for parts unknown, but Booger held onto his leash and, with barely a whimper, he gave up the chase.

Wizzie laughed, and the sound grew contagious. Roger Eagle chuckled and Billy wheezed.

Booger shook his head. "I think I just had a heart attack," he said, and Wizzie laughed some more.

Later, when the guests were gone and Billy was in his "man cave" watching his favorite hunting show, Wizzie sat alone on the porch. The dishes were clean and the glasses were, too, but the candles still flickered and she sat and stared into the dark, and wondered what she was waiting for.

She feared the red glow that signaled the ghosts of spirits past, and yet a part of her had always felt safer when Red Wolf or Tala was around. She knew Booger felt the same, and wondered if they hadn't doomed the two to a horrible afterlife in trying to rid themselves of Chief Running Blood.

The night ticked on, but Wizzie felt no comfort in the flickering flames that surrounded her. She wondered if there would ever come a time when she would believe they were at peace, or safe from the spirits that haunted their world.

She doubted it. *What other spirits lurked out there?* she wondered. *And how long until they realized she, her husband and their friends could see them?*

Epilogue

Booger awoke in the middle of the night, sheets twisted around his legs. They were damp, like the rest of him, and his heart pounded as sweat drizzled from his forehead and stung his blinking eyes.

He sat up, the room dark around him, and listened closely for the sound that had roused him from a restless sleep. It had been a wolf howling softly in the night, a low, unforgiving sound, anxious, bold and vengeful.

He heard nothing except for the pumping of blood coursing through his own veins. And then there it was again. He looked frantically for a red glow outside his window. But there was nothing, only Budweiser lying in the corner, teeth bared, snout quivering, having a dog's bad dream.

The growl was soft and fuzzy and Booger sighed out loud with relief. "Budweiser," he said softly to himself as the dog whimpered in the corner, muscles flexing beneath his soft and shiny coat. "You old —"

And then came the sound…the low and unmistakable sound of a wolf—a real wolf—howling in the night. Booger whimpered and yet stole from his sheets, dragging them off the bed as he untangled himself crudely on the way to the window.

He threw up the sash, expecting the warm, familiar red glow that announced Tala's presence. But it was nowhere to be seen. Instead the air was still and damp, dew forming on the grass that led to Wolf Creek.

The howl grew louder with the window open, though try as he might Booger couldn't see a hint of a fiery red glow or even fur. He slipped over the ledge and onto the grass, his bare feet cold on in the early morning dew as he crept quietly toward the riverbank.

A soft mist rolled across the creek but nothing rose from it, no man nor beast nor ghost nor spirit. Weary but wide awake, Booger sank onto the bank and watched, and waited, for something— anything—to happen.

Finally, he heard creeping and, turning slightly to his left, saw a familiar face, troubled with concern.

"Booger!" said Wizzie. "What's that noise?"

He patted the ground next to him as Wizzie approached, hands clenched tight around the sash of her favorite maroon robe. "You know what it is." He chuckled humorlessly as she sat next to him. "Or you wouldn't be out here with me at three in the morning!"

She groaned but looked as wide awake as he was. Together they sat, well into the night and close to the dawn, listening for the sound of the wolf's howl and, every so often, being rewarded with its low, menacing growl.

"But where is it?" she asked, turning to him. "Why can't we see it?"

"Maybe it's not Tala," Booger said. "Maybe it's just some random wolf out there in the dark, and we'll never, ever see it."

"Let's hope so," Wizzie said, nodding, though like him she made no move to leave. Instead they sat longer and longer, waiting for the red glow to come. It came, but only at sunrise as the water rippled orange and, for a moment, red.

"You better get to school," said Wizzie, patting his knee as he struggled to his feet.

"What are you going to do?" he asked, since she hadn't followed him to stand up.

"Just sit here for a little longer," she said, smiling up at him, the orange glow of sunrise kind on her face. "See if our old friends show up."

"And if they do?" he asked, a note of concern in his voice.

She slid a cell phone from one robe pocket, wielding it like a weapon. "I've got Roger Eagle's number on speed dial," she said. "Yours and Billy's, too."

He nodded and turned away, taking one last look at the riverbank before creeping to his window. As she sat there, hunched into herself, hands clutching her arms in the early morning chill, he wasn't sure if Wizzie was afraid that Tala might be the one howling in the night…or hopeful that it could be.

Climbing back in his window, Booger wasn't sure which way he felt either. And maybe he never would.

Read on for a sneak peek at *Red Mahogany*, book two in

The Tala Chronicles:

Dark Sunglasses watches her through his Nikon DLX-Digicam as the sun sets on the banks of Wolf Creek. His black truck is parked under the canopy of trees next to the large row of hedges located at the side of the Franks' home. He lays the camera on the truck seat next to him and pulls out the photos he took two days ago.

He smacks the steering wheel with his hand. *Damn it*, he thinks. *The red glare is in these photos, too.* He picks up his camera again, cleans the lens and points it toward the house and Wizzie.

"Mmm," he murmurs and licks his lips. Click, click, click. Then he rolls the window down, sticks the camera out, and points it toward the house and Wizzie again. Click, click, click.

He watches as she points the remote toward the TV and the exercise channel comes to life. People on the TV screen bop back and forth and Wizzie follows, her ponytail whipping from side to side. She bends and stretches with her butt in the air, and stomps her feet, her hips swaying back and forth and her large breasts jiggling as she moves.

He drools as he watches her. *I will have my pleasure with you, Ms. Wizzie Frank, and I will take my time before I kill you.*

ABOUT THE AUTHOR

Toni House is an entrepreneur, novelist and mother. She began writing and reading stories at an early age, but as time went on, put her writing on hold until 2009 when she published her first non-fiction self-help book. Her second non-fiction self-help book was published in 2010. Her true love is writing and telling stories that readers will love and want to read more. Her first fiction novel, *The Song of The Red Wolf,* is based loosely on true events. It is the first in a three-book series. She also plans to publish a spinoff novel, *Winter Snow,* about a Native American princess. Toni lives in the southern United States with her family and two of the sweetest fur babies on the planet.

Events:

Monthly book giveaways ToniHouseAuthor.com

Goodreads.com

National Book Signings: ToniHouseAuthor.com

Radio Station Interviews: ToniHouseAuthor.com

To Schedule an Interview Contact:

MarketingSourceBooks@gmail.com